Gorgon's Price

Cover Design: Kanaxa
Editor: Angela Sanders
Formatting: Jacob Hammer

Claire Davon
P.O. Box 731
Van Nuys, CA 91408

Print ISBN: 978-1-946621-15-3
Digital ISBN: 978-1-946621-14-6

First Digital Publication: December 2019
First Print Publication: December, 2019

Gorgon's Price

Claire Davon

Dedication

To all of you who go on these journeys with me. I appreciate you more than you know!

Acknowledgments

This book was originally written as part of a box set. When that box set started to fall apart those of us in the set were fortunate to have each other's support while we figured out our next move. While I was sorry that the box set didn't happen, it did give me this terrific book. I could not have been so sure of my decision to withdraw from the set and publish this book on my own without their help, and I thank each and every one of them (you know who you are)!

Also to the Shark Club and The Coven, who I can turn to for issues, problems and advice. This crazy year would not have gone nearly as well without your friendship.

Of course thank you to my readers, who go with me on these rides to faraway places and encounter many wondrous beings. I hope you enjoy this take on the Gorgons as much as I enjoyed writing about them!

Chapter One

For the first time in millennia, Euryale woke up without a head of snakes.

Her ears registered the quiet. Since they had been transformed into monsters by Athena so long ago, she had spent every waking moment—and some sleeping ones—with the sound of hissing. Now the silence settled around her like a blanket, soft and low and a little unnerving.

After all this time, she was alone. Her snakes didn't have sentience, but they had life and moved according to their whims. Now they were gone, along with the other manifestations of a goddess's displeasure.

Scrambling up, she dashed to the bathroom and grabbed the hand mirror— that was the one reflection she allowed herself. Euryale, or Elexis as some called her, felt her head, unable to believe it. Nothing moved. Euryale dropped the hand mirror and yanked the sheet off the larger one. It, like all other reflective surfaces in the place, was covered.

It had been thousands of years since she'd seen her face in anything more than a rare glimpse. She studied her hand. When she'd gone to bed last night, it had been tipped in claws, but now it was like any other hand. She turned it over. The back was cracked and in need of moisturizer, but it was skin and not scales.

Her cell phone rang, startling her. She knew who it was before she reached for the device.

"Stheno," she said after she pressed the speaker. "Has it happened to you as well?" She wanted to leap for joy but that would send her miles up. Or would it? Perhaps she didn't have her power. But that would be stupid. Ares would not have offered her this bargain if he had taken away her powers. That was the whole point.

"Yes," her older, firstborn sister said, displeasure in her voice. "Sister, I told you not to do it. You cannot trust the gods."

Euryale had agreed for each of them but hadn't been certain how Stheno would feel in the end. Of the three, she had embraced their monstrous aspects, and used them to her advantage in battle.

"You agreed," Euryale said, her back stiffening. "You, too, desired a human appearance."

Stheno, or Saskia, as she was called to those who did not know her, snorted into the phone.

"Whether I did or not, I warned you about trusting the gods." She exhaled a long breath. "But it is done. We have taken a human form once again. We still have our powers, which I believe was part of your bargain. I am a warrior; if it had been otherwise, I would have never agreed. If they had not been good to their word, I would already be on my way to Mount Olympus to confront them. You will have to test for yourself, but most should be intact. It is your hair and skin that have transformed, that is all. You are—we are—no longer monsters."

Euryale released a sigh. She translated Stheno's words in her mind. Bastards. Yes, the Greek gods were bastards.

"It will take some time to get used to the shift."

"Just as it did when that bitch Athena changed us. She should have turned on her rapist brother Poseidon, instead she took it out on us."

"As is often true of the gods. They stick to their own. We are but poor descendants of those they would rather forget."

"Our parents are descended from Gaia and gods in their own right."

"But we are monsters."

"We are not monsters anymore, Sister." Stheno paused for a moment. "While I dislike what you did to achieve this, I do have to admit, it will be nice to be able to move in society without concealment."

This was as close to a "thank you" as she was going to get.

Stheno was in Egypt, where modest clothing and head coverings was not uncommon. Euryale beheld her Wyoming home. She had chosen the United States for many reasons, but paramount among them was the cold climate where she could be bundled up much of the year. The rest of the time she wore scarves.

"Euryale," Stheno said and paused. The line crackled around them; the connection iffy. She would not ask where Stheno was and doubted that her sister would tell her. She often operated in secrecy. If she needed Euryale to know, she would tell her.

"Yes, Sister?"

There was another pause and Stheno took a breath. The sound echoed through the line, full of portents and meaning.

"I will go to Medusa," Stheno said finally. "I will ascertain if she is changed. That cave in Sumeria, now Iraq, should be safe enough, but who is to say what could happen if she awakens from her stasis. You take the gods, and I will deal with our sister."

Although mortal, Medusa had been gifted with a piece of her sibling's immortality. She would not live forever, and had spent years in stasis until her sisters were able to smuggle her head back to her after Perseus cut it off. Medusa, the prettiest of the three, did not take the change well. It was safer for her to remain asleep.

"Thank you. I could not do both tasks. Once this is over, and I have dealt with the gods, will you shed your burka and come visit me?"

Saskia snorted. "I do not wear a burka. I wear a hijab. Perhaps I will come later, but I have work here. I must rearrange things to go to Medusa. Let's video conference next week when I have more time. I am on assignment at the moment. I had to call you, though, and check on you. I am not certain that I'm not still angry with you for going around me, but it is done."

"Do you mind so much being human in appearance again?'

Again, the rushing sound before Stheno emitted a short laugh.

"No. You are right about that. Only, be careful, my impulsive sister. Bargains with the gods rarely turn out well."

"I understand that. I will watch my back. Let's talk soon."

Euryale hung up the phone, gave her reflection one more glance, and began her morning routine.

It was a relief that her sister was not angrier. When she had told Stheno of Ares's proposal, her sister had flatly refused. It had taken several calls for her to consider the idea, which Euryale, the "far roaming" one, if you went by Greek mythology, had taken as assent. At first, she was going to refuse the arrogant Greek god, and would have walked away from his image over video conference, but he had waved his hand, and she found she could not hang up the phone. When he laid out his proposal, she gaped at him.

"You mean to turn us back into the likeness of humans? In exchange for, what again?"

The god, in the form of a muscular youth with curling black hair and a long beard, sighed and studied her, his expression enigmatic.

"You must seek out a person or group who is killing gods. If you agree, I will have Athena turn you back permanently."

"Killing gods? You?"

He waved a hand with a desultory air, but she couldn't help but note it trembled as he did so.

"Not major pantheons, of course, few have that power. We need someone the group won't expect, and there are few who meet that criteria. Say yes, and I will ensure the curse you and your sisters have been burdened with for millennia is lifted."

The idea of still being immortal, without her curse again filled Euryale with a strange mixture of hope and dismay. She stared at the god.

"I have a few conditions before I agree," she said. "Assuming I do."

Ares inclined his head. "Of course you do. What are they?"

He was the war god, well used to battle, but left the negotiating to others. He was the bloody one, who charged in and slaughtered. She appreciated him for that. Over her millennia as a monster, she had slain many and turned hundreds to stone.

"This change applies to all of us, myself and my sisters."

Ares shook his head. "Not Medusa."

Euryale clacked her teeth together, exposing her fangs. To his credit, Ares didn't blanch, nor did he stare at the snakes hissing around her head. Normally she would tell them to be quiet, but she encouraged them to writhe around her face for this call. "Yes. Especially her. All of us or none. I have been this way forever, Ares—what makes you think I am eager to return to my human form?"

She would never disclose to Ares how she longed for the feel of skin and not scales. Hair and not snakes. Her heart beat faster at the idea of looking human once again. She turned away so her feelings would not show. One snake stuck out his tongue, hissing in counterpart to her breath.

He sighed, and even through the image, it was apparent he was displeased. "Very well. It will make it harder for me to persuade Athena to agree."

"All or none," she repeated.

"Agreed."

"I want to keep my powers. And my sisters' as well."

He shook his head. "Most of them, yes. You would do us little good if you were frail. You will not have the capacity to fight gods if you are merely human. But you cannot turn men to stone with a glare."

She considered. "Then I want the ability to do so if needed. I, and my sisters, will keep our other abilities. My voice. My capability to jump. Stheno's strength and talent for killing."

"You may have those—you *must* have those. The remainder we will have to consider. I am uncertain if I can grant you the ability to turn others to stone in human form. Perhaps as needed. I am already at my limit with Athena. I cannot say yes to this request without further discussion. Do not ask more of me."

She began to argue, but the idea of no longer being a monster stilled her voice. She recognized when a god had been pushed to their limit. Even all these centuries later, one did not forget the day they had been turned into a beast.

Euryale inclined her head. Her voice was as sibilant as a snake's when she spoke again, fear and rising excitement warring within her. "I don't like it, so try to get those as well. For now, Ares, I agree to your terms. I will help you fight this new threat to the pantheon. But first, you must ensure that my sisters have been granted the same boon."

There was silence for several moments, and then Ares's voice came back on the line.

"It is done. You will wait for further instructions. There will be another contacting you regarding your next steps. He will be your partner in this. Do not fail us, Euryale, or…do not fail." He signed off, leaving Euryale grimacing at the phone with her restored face.

She didn't want a partner, but she was not given a choice. However, if he was someone she couldn't work with, she would soon discover just how much of her glare she'd retained.

* * *

"Man, I don't know how you get that sound."

"Do we have what we need?" Asher said, his chin sinking to his chest. After twelve hours in the sound booth, he was ready to go home.

The producer gave a wave of his hand. "All good, man. I need you next week for overdubbing. Until then, I'm done with you. I couldn't do it without you, man. Damn. That shit is eerie."

Asher snapped off the headphones and placed them on the stand. Then he stepped out from the voiceover booth and went to where the producer was looping back his sounds.

His lucrative job doing vocal sound effects put his peculiar heritage and talents to work while still keeping a low profile.

Having a banshee mother was good for something. It gave him a range that allowed him to use his voice to good effect in the horror genre. Many sounds these days were done via computer, but his variety let them add a human touch. After five years in the business, he was highly sought after.

"Great. I've got a date with a mountain. Time to get some climbing done."

Jimmy patted his slight belly. "Have fun with that. Just don't strain that voice of yours. I need it to imitate an alien being gutted by a space vampire."

Asher laughed. "Same ole, same ole."

* * *

His phone rang while he was in the car and Asher glanced at the number. It was an International call, starting with 353, which meant Ireland. That meant it was likely to be his mother. Asher's brows pulled together and his mouth twitched. This was unusual; he'd just talked to her a few days ago. He debated letting it go to voice mail, but another part of him thumbed the phone to accept the call and set it to video.

"Hello, Mother. This is a surprise."

The woman with long hair and a grey cloak, draped over a green dress, studied Asher for a long moment, saying nothing. He didn't understand why his mother chose to come to him wearing the folklore version of her clothing, but that was a banshee for you. It told him without words that something was wrong.

"Cop on, son," she said. "I'm not coddling you now. The time has come."

Asher blinked at the figure on his screen. Of all the calls he'd been dreading, this was top of the list.

"What do you mean?" He knew full well what she meant—but on the slight off chance it was something else, he didn't want to jinx it. He'd learned many things over the years, and one was that you didn't put something out in the universe unless you were ready for it to come true.

"I was gobsmacked when he called, but Ares has claimed his favor." Her voice was shrill, and it didn't take much to translate that into a wail. That was what banshees did, after all. True, it didn't take the form that the tales indicated, but some of the legends were accurate.

"It's not a good time, Mother. I'm about to go out with a group of friends and spend three days on a mountainside. Can it wait?"

There was the beginning of a shriek in her words. He would have covered his ears, but he was in thick Los Angeles traffic and couldn't take his hands off the wheel.

"Don't make a hash of this, Asher. I'm serious."

"Sorry, sorry," he muttered, and she subsided. "We were aware this day would come, but I hoped he would forget."

She threw her hood back and laughed. Contrary to legends, banshees were not old hags who were withered and gaunt. Or if they were, it was by choice to scare those they had come to haunt. In her natural guise, his mother resembled a plump middle-aged woman, with pleasant Irish features and thick red hair.

He'd inherited his appearance from his father, the Greek god, Ares. Roisin had wanted a son and managed to convince Ares to help her with that quest. Banshees had seldom, if ever, been male, but with the god's assistance, Roisin had gotten her wish. In exchange, Ares reserved the right to use her son for a favor, to be called in at a time of his choosing. In the hundred years Asher had been alive, Ares had never contacted them. Now his luck had run out.

"What does he want? A river diverted? For me to go down to Hades and retrieve a lute? Steal something from another pantheon? What is the errand?"

His mother's chest heaved at Asher's mocking tone. Behind her, the chirping birds went silent.

"You sound flummoxed, but a hundred years is nothing to a god. Your birthday was yesterday, like, to him. He put the heart crossways to me when he rang; I thought I'd have more time before he remembered you. He wasn't slagging, he needs you."

Parking the car in front of his West Hollywood home, Asher left the engine running. He turned to face her, a muscle jumping in the back of his jaw.

"What do you mean? They're deities. Immortal. How can they be in need?"

"It's very savage-like. Someone is killing gods. You've got to find the moran and stop him. You can't make a bag of this. Ares teamed you up with Euryale—she will be your partner."

"Who is Euryale?"

"Medusa's sister. One of the immortal Gorgons."

Asher burst out laughing. "Has Ares hit his head?"

"The skinny is that he made Athena turn them into women again. You must partner with Euryale in this. Volunteers are scarce as hen's teeth, so here we are. Once the gods are dead, it takes years for them to come back to life." She paused. "It is brock, son. The Tuatha dé Danann have not been…unaffected."

He digested the idea that the pantheon that included the Queen of the Banshees had been affected. "You didn't tell me that. Is Clíodhna okay?"

Roisin nodded. "Aye. It is not our queen who was harmed. Don't have a puss. You must do this, Asher. You know the contract."

"How am I supposed to get a Gorgon to do anything? What am I supposed to do?"

Damn it. He'd been anticipating a few days of relaxing downtime, and now he had to deal with the fucking Greek pantheon.

"This may be murder for you, but you have no choice. Remember the bargain."

"This is *not* a good time. What if I refuse?"

As soon as he said it, Asher recognized his mistake. His mother opened her mouth and let out a wail so piercing, it blared through his speakers, filling the cabin of his SUV with the racket.

Then she cut it off and pointed a finger at him.

"Don't be annoying me. You are not a mog, or an oath breaker. If you fail, you can at best expect a visit from Adrestia, daughter of Ares, in punishment for your hubris. The worst is that Ares would act as he said he would if we did not fulfill the pact. If you leg it, my son, one or both of us will die. Aye, I do not care for myself, but male banshees are rare as hen's teeth. You are my boy and I would protect you."

Asher swallowed, beads of sweat prickling on the back of his neck. He shivered, although it was warm in the car. His mother had insulted him several times in the space of the short conversation, something she never did.

"Surely Ares wouldn't…"

Roisin let out a bitter laugh, the banshee wail just behind the harsh tones.

"He may not be the full shilling, but he is a god. You've got to give it a lash, son. You cannot fail. What is done cannot be undone. You do a bunk and you doom both of us. Wait for Ares to ring. Do as he tells you. *Slán.*"

With the Gaelic word for goodbye ringing in his ears, Asher pressed the "Off" button on his Smartphone.

He sat in his car, drumming his hands on the steering wheel. Just like that, with one word from an absent father, who was also a major Greek god, Asher's life had been turned upside down.

"Fuck!" He banged his hand on the dashboard, aware it was futile.

Before he was born, a bargain had been struck, and he now had to fulfill it, whatever it took. His life hung in the balance.

Chapter Two

Taking up a fighting stance, Euryale flung the door open after the doorbell had been rung once, and then a second time.

The man in front of her stood around six four and was too handsome to be human. There was something about the paranormal that radiated, whether they were gods, monsters, or supernatural. This one had the air of the divine, who could change their aspect as it suited them and be as gorgeous—or as ugly—as they desired. He was attractive in a traditional way: rugged, clean cut, and broad shouldered. Euryale retreated from the door, adrenaline surging through her veins for more than one reason.

"I assume you're here to talk about Ares," she said. If he wasn't who she thought he was, she would usher him out as fast as she'd let him in.

"Yes," he said and stepped inside. He kicked the door shut with a single foot, leaving the light swirling snow outside. Euryale shivered when the cold touched her. For all the millennia as a monster, she hadn't worried about the weather.

"I'm Elexis," she said but didn't offer her hand.

"Asher," he said and extended his. She stared at it for a moment and then shook what was offered. Her hand no longer had scales and the sight of her olive-tinted skin—similar in complexion to his—still startled her. It was going to take a while to get used to the change.

"What qualifies you for this mission, Asher?" She could feel her talent lurking in her vocal cords, a humming similar to her snakes.

"I'm part banshee, part god. You were one of the Gorgons until recently. Euryale, even though you introduced yourself as Elexis. Is that true?"

"I was a Gorgon before Athena changed us and I remain one today. Euryale is my true name but it's too distinctive, so I go by Elexis. Word travels fast."

His eyes were a deep chocolate brown, with gold flecks dancing in the irises. He had black hair with brown highlights. He would command attention anywhere, with his height and muscular build.

For a moment she wished she hadn't made the bargain with Ares. At least as a monster she knew where she stood. Now everything was new. Still, when she caught him giving her an appraising stare, she understood there were advantages to being human.

"Banshees are female."

He took off his gloves and slapped them against his jeans, drawing her attention to his powerful thighs. Her old self would rend and claw at him, demanding coupling. A new, more gentle emotion stirred inside her. Euryale controlled the urge to stare.

"Banshees *are* female," he agreed. "My mother wanted a boy child, something few banshees had, and went in search of a willing god. Ares was that deity. But he laid conditions on this gift. A task, at a time of his choosing. So here I am." The strain in his voice told her there was more to the story, but she didn't press. It wasn't necessary to be his friend, and she didn't want to invite confidences. This was a job, nothing more.

He was a demigod, but not any more in control of his destiny than she was. Somehow it made him more acceptable.

"Is that how you were born, or did you change your appearance to be more attractive to women...or men...or whatever you are into?"

He shrugged out of his coat and she saw that her initial assessment had not deceived her. His shoulders were broad, his chest defined, the entire bundle enough to make even gods stop and take a second glimpse. He would be a compelling package even without his divine blood.

His grin was brief, but sincere. "It's all me. My mother had a hand in it, I'm sure. She's never admitted it to me, but some of my aunties tell me that she went to Clíodhna to ensure that I would be handsome."

"And did the Queen of the Banshees grant her request?" Euryale would be damned if she revealed to Asher that he was gorgeous. Beauty among gods was easy, integrity and trustworthiness, much more difficult.

"You tell me." His smile might have been genuine, but it was hard to tell.

"Not a chance. Fill me in on what you can."

* * *

Asher refused to stare at the woman in the passenger seat of the jet. Of all the things he'd thought on the plane ride up here, the idea that he would find one of the fearsome Gorgons attractive hadn't occurred to him. He imagined that she would still retain some evidence of her centuries of monsterhood, but she was pretty, with curly brown hair and eyes the color of a summer storm. She should've been a daughter of Artemis. He would *not* say those words out loud. He doubted the Gorgon had any love for the major Greek pantheon.

"What should we do when we get back to Los Angeles?"

Euryale's attention was focused out the window, but he could see her reflection. She met his gaze, something that came easier to her than meeting it face-to-face.

When your stare could turn people to stone, he supposed it became natural to keep it averted.

"We assemble supplies," he said. "We come up with a plan. I haven't the faintest, Elexis. I was drafted, I didn't volunteer."

"What have you been told so far?"

"There is someone or a group of 'someones' killing gods," he said, and the words sounded strange even to him. "At first it didn't cause any waves. They started small, on some of the obscure pantheons who were dying out anyway, but then they became bolder."

"You mean, the old ones who nobody worships anymore?"

He nodded. "Yes."

She kept her gaze fixed on the horizon. "Those deities remained dead?"

He made a seesaw motion with his hand. "It's unclear. There are some that exist in scraps of stories and some of those groups can't be located. But it's possible they faded away, as others have when humans stop believing in them. Then this group, whoever they are, moved on to bigger game. Verbti from the Albanian pantheon went missing. It went unnoticed."

"Oh, the arrogance of the major gods," she muttered. "If you're not Greek, Roman, Norse, Egyptian, or the Christian god, then you are nobody."

He inclined his head. "True. Then these 'someones' started going after our minor gods and immortals, and we began to stir."

"By 'we,' I presume you mean the Greeks and not the banshees?"

He nodded. "Banshees are long-lived but not eternal."

"You're safe then."

He wished he knew what she was thinking, but her mental shields were so powerful, he couldn't glimpse into her mind at all.

"That remains to be seen. The first of the pantheons have resurrected but some are still dead."

She turned from the window and met his gaze. His cock stirred at the sight of her troubled grey eyes peering at him. Her hands clenched on the armrests of the six-passenger jet.

Damn it, this timing sucked. If it hadn't been his life, or worse, his mother's life on the line, he would have told Ares to take a hike. He had a job to do and no time to waste. Luckily, he didn't have a girlfriend—that would have been difficult to explain—but this disruption had come at a horrible time. Still, there was nothing to be done. You didn't say no to the gods, especially when they held your life in the balance. His career, he could put back together, but not his mother. He didn't like it—at all—but that was the shit sandwich he'd been handed.

"I feel sorry for the older pantheons; they have no method of defense. The Greeks, too bad for them. Arrogant bastards. Nice that something can take them down from their high-and-mighty perch." Her face had a crumpled quality, her eyes glittering grey icicles. "How are they being killed?"

"It's not completely clear, but from what I've been told, they think it has something to do with sound and sound vibrations."

"Hence a banshee and a Gorgon with a voice," she mused. "How long will they stay dead?"

"Ares didn't say. I'm not sure."

"It's relevant. They should tell us. What else are they keeping from us?"

Asher shifted his gaze away, pressing his hands together. The Gorgon returned her focus on a point outside the window, and he found—to his surprise—he coveted a glance from those grey orbs again. Grey. The color of the stone she could once turn men into. He should run far away from her.

He turned to her but couldn't determine her expression. "They went after Nereus and almost succeeded in killing him. They failed, but it was close."

She whistled. "The old man of the sea and the god of fish. Not quite a major god, but pretty close. Figures, the Greeks would only care when it came to one of their own. They didn't manage their goal, so why are the gods afraid?"

* * *

He paused and Euryale wondered if he was going to answer.

"Have you seen Raijin lately?"

She shook her head, her eyebrows drawing together at this non-sequitur. "I have never met that Japanese god of lightning and storms. Even if I had, until yesterday I was not in the habit of consorting with gods."

When he met her gaze, his regard was a bit rueful. "Sorry, Elexis, I keep forgetting. I can't imagine…anyway, it's said that Raijin was killed. If they succeeded with the Japanese pantheon, there's nothing to say they couldn't achieve it with the Greeks. It's too soon to tell if he'll resurrect or not."

She drummed her fingertips on the armrest. Around them, the thrum of the engines was muted but still present. As a Gorgon she had to fly from time to time, and the glamour that shielded the paranormal truth from the rest of the world held even on planes, but she was always careful not to let others touch her. While their monstrous aspect could be hidden, she learned through the years that the feel of her scales alerted humans that there was something *different* about her, even if they didn't have the insight to discern the truth. More than one of those unwary folk had died before they could find out. Monsters did what monsters had to do.

"That's why the Greek pantheon is concerned."

"Of course. If the major gods go down, it could cause a power struggle in Olympus and disrupt the delicate balance there for far longer than the god's resurrection would account for. Whoever these people are, they need to be stopped. Anarchy and chaos would ensue."

"Some might say that a ruthless god, like Zeus, could use that kind of weapon for their own purposes." *Or a ruthless Gorgon.*

"I would think even Zeus isn't immune."

Or Athena. Euryale's belief stayed shuttered behind her shields. She checked them again to make sure no hint had slipped out. Euryale had a pact with Ares, but that didn't mean her sister Stheno was held to that pledge. There may come a day when the power of the sisters could be used to gain revenge on the goddess who had condemned all the Gorgons to their terrible fate. Stheno hadn't said as much, but Euryale suspected her warrior sister would not forget the insult to the Gorgons. Time would tell.

"What makes them think we will have better luck stopping this than a god?"

Asher's broad shoulders twitched against the trendy form-fitting shirt he was wearing. The ripple of his muscles was evident under the cloth, and something flipped inside her belly. It had been a long time since she had been driven by anything other than bestial desires. If she were in her other form, she would have sniffed the air to inspect if he was feeling the same heat she was. But she was no longer a beast.

Except she was. It had taken them decades to stop thinking of themselves as immortal goddesses, and it would also be the reverse. It had been so long since someone considered her with longing—and for her to feel that same pulse within her—Euryale wasn't sure what to make of it.

"How much do you grasp of how things work today?"

She scoffed at him. "I'm a monster, but I'm not living in a cave. That's for legends. I made my home in Casper, Wyoming after all. I can function—I have a glamour that allows me to move in human circles. I keep to myself and don't socialize, but I get by. I can assure you I act appropriately in polite company. I'm not going to turn around and eat them. Although," she grinned and allowed her shields to slip, "mortals can be tasty."

The image she projected of eating a man who had mistaken her human form for a weak one was designed to shock. To Asher's credit, he displayed no emotion.

"Good. That will make this easier." Euryale was disappointed. He took her for who she was now and not a monster, something she hadn't experienced in a long time.

"What do you have in mind?"

"Our cover is that I met you when I vacationed here last, and we fell in love. It's been a long-distance relationship. You're moving to Los Angeles to live with me. To answer your question, I think the reason that the gods asked for our help is because we can find out things a god could not. We're both creatures whose weapons are sound, and it may come in handy in battle."

Euryale met his gaze and tried to probe his mind but found that his shields were good. Almost, but not quite as good as hers.

"Asher, that's nonsense. The real reason they came to us is that we are expendable."

He nodded. "That too."

Chapter Three

The Gorgon wasn't what he'd expected. In the hundred years he'd been alive, he'd come to understand that gods and monsters alike were mostly made up of tales that had been passed down over time and not reality. His family was proof of that. The banshees were not just those who wailed over the upcoming deaths of certain Irish families, but a living, breathing culture of their own. He should've been aware that the same was true of Euryale.

He watched her take inventory of his Spanish-style West Hollywood home and wished he could read her better. He was no slouch among women, but this one didn't behave like the others he was accustomed to. If she flirted, he could deal with that. If she wielded power like a weapon, he could handle that, as well. She did neither, just took in her surroundings and cataloged them for future use.

"I keep forgetting you had scales and snakes two days ago."

Her head snapped up and her face tightened. She'd been in the process of examining a cactus on the ledge, but then she swerved to face him. At her glare, Asher backed up a step, believing in that moment, she could turn men to stone. Legends varied on whether or not the three sisters each had that power, but he was now certain that, at one point, Euryale had been able to. He prayed she no longer had the ability. If she did, he'd be a statue decorating his home by now.

"*Oipho*, banshee, I don't need reminders of what I was. I would appreciate it if you would leave that in the past. If you persist on calling me a monster, then we're going to have an issue."

He had no idea what the word "Oipho" meant, but the meaning was clear. Asher raised his hands. "I meant no offense. You were a Gorgon before you were changed to a beast, so is it okay to call you that?'

Her countenance took several moments to clear before she nodded.

"Yes. Gorgons are still associated with fiends and may forever be so. You are right, however. It was, and is, who we are."

"Gorgon it is, then. Do I call you Elexis or Euryale?"

"Elexis is my 'human' name, but it is probably better to use that than to try and remember to call me Euryale in private and Elexis in public. It is up to you. I will answer to either."

He took a step closer, and to his relief, she didn't scowl. She was a touchy one, but he was used to strong women. She didn't scare him. Well…maybe a little. Her curly hair wasn't hard to imagine coiled into snakes. Her skin, while just skin now, showed signs of being ill taken care of, still resembling scales in its flaky dryness. Not that he would tell her that, of course. He valued his limbs.

She wouldn't be some preening miss like so many of the women here in Los Angeles. This woman was a warrior. He wouldn't have to watch her back. She was likely a better fighter than he was. Perhaps that was another reason the gods had selected her to join this cause.

"Monsters have a bad reputation. Some consider my mother's clan of women, the banshees, to be freaks as well. It's because they alert humans that death is coming. That scares them, so they refer to the messenger as a fiend."

Euryale's shoulders relaxed, and Asher released a covert breath.

"Some believe that we deserved the fate thrust upon us by Athena."

He cocked his head, a silent request to continue.

"The legends indicate that because Medusa was a priestess, that Athena had the right to be angry when Medusa was defiled by Poseidon in her temple. As if a mortal could win a battle with a god. Even a mortal goddess had no chance against one of the major pantheons. Some think that we should not have stood by our sister, but we would not let her face her fate alone. The gods were unfair to us, but none more than Medusa. All three of us paid the price, but she was the one who was dealt the highest cost."

Asher considered his next words with care. "You're sisters, descended from gods. How is it that she's mortal?"

Euryale's gaze said she wouldn't tell him one way or the other. "The ways of the gods are strange. We are immortal, she was not. I don't understand why. She is so beautiful. Some say that that is the tradeoff. She was given excessive beauty, and therefore could not be eternal."

"Yet, it's said she's still alive?"

Euryale made a vague gesture with her hands that might have been indecision. "She is protected. Stheno and I cannot keep her from dying, but we have been able to slow down her aging by keeping her in stasis much of the time. Someday she will die permanently."

"How did you resurrect her after Perseus cut off her head?"

Euryale clucked her tongue. "That is a tale for another day. Your home will be sufficient for our needs. How do we start our quest?"

* * *

Saturday found Asher at the gym, working out with his friend, Lenno. To most, Lenno was a Native American man with black hair that fell below his shoulders and light brown skin. He was also paranormal; in his case, he was Mishipeshu: The Water-Panther. Often described as a giant dragon-like feline, the most common element was the monster's aquatic habitat; it lurked in lakes and rivers, waiting for the unwary to come close to the water, then drowned them. He was even said to have a snaky, prehensile tail that aided in snaring its prey.

Just as so many other legends were meant to scare people, the folklore of the Mishipeshu was no different. Lenno was a formidable man, and Asher was sure he was twice as terrifying in his panther shape. He'd never observed Lenno's other form, but he had no reason to doubt it. The myths didn't exist without a reason.

They had been friends for five years, almost since Asher first arrived in Los Angeles. It felt like he'd been friends with Lenno for most of the century he'd been alive. He was a guy; he didn't have best friends. Lenno came close. He discounted the idea that the Mishipeshu was a monster, just as Euryale wasn't a monster—anymore, anyway. Lenno may be fierce, but he wasn't without reason.

They were sparring in the practice ring of the gym. It was not only a good way to let out aggression, but a great way to meet and talk without raising suspicion. Their pattern was well established and had been that way for years. Today would cause no red flags.

"Gorgon, you say?" Lenno said, dancing around Asher and trying to land punches, which Asher blocked.

"Yeah. She's still a Gorgon, but not a monster anymore. They let her keep many of her powers, though."

Lenno gave Asher a cool appraisal. "You'd better hope she didn't retain the turning to stone part. That could be a problem."

Asher laughed and jabbed at Lenno in return. "Not that, so far, anyway. I'd already be yard art, I fear." She was different from any other woman he'd met. She shied away from physical touch like his skin was going to reach out and bite her.

"Why her? Why the two of you? If it's sound related, there are a lot of banshees and others in this world with the same kind of power: Sirens. The Nue birds of China. They didn't have to go get a male banshee and a freaking Gorgon."

"The Nue goes 'nyoo nyoo.' I don't think it would be effective. Same with the Fenghuang. It has to be sound related, so I agree with you. What the others have wouldn't get it done. Sirens, yeah, they might have worked, but I don't get the impression they're all that eager to help the gods. They're not their favorites." He paused and then started boxing with Lenno again. "Besides, I owe them, and I don't have a choice. Eur…Elexis, too."

After several moments of silent fighting, Lenno spoke, "If you say so. Why the hell is she staying with you? She was a monster a week ago. How can you trust her? She doesn't lose centuries of instincts overnight. She might eat you in your sleep."

Asher punched at Lenno for a few moments. The gym was sparsely populated this time of night. At near eleven, they had the place to themselves, except for the bored custodian in the corner and one person skipping rope. It was the perfect time for the duo.

"I can't trust her, Lenno, and I don't. We have a job to do, that's all. After we're done, then I'll cut her loose."

"What happens if you don't succeed? I can't imagine the gods will be pleased if you fail. They may turn you into a monster as well."

Asher's face paled, but otherwise, he didn't display any other outward signs of emotion to his friend—he hoped. "Quite possible. That's what happens when you bargain with the gods." He stopped sparring and dropped his arms. "Mom left me a sweet little legacy that I have to close out. If we fail…well, we won't fail. We can't."

Lenno raised his hands and took a jab at Asher. It connected, and Asher let out a "whuff" of surprise.

"Got it. No failure. Now, let's spar again."

Asher left out the part about finding Euryale's curves and her overall air of tragic loneliness a beacon to him. As a male banshee with no counterpart and a man who was half god, he didn't fit in anywhere. Paranormals like his friend, those descended from myth and legend, had power and strength of their history to draw on. He, Asher, was an anomaly, and the supernatural world didn't like those. His last friend, a shifter mountain lion named Rafe, had suggested he contact the man when he arrived in Los Angeles. When he'd done so, Asher had found a soul akin to his own. It hadn't taken long for the two unlikely friends to bond.

Once they were done, Asher went to towel off and change. As he did, he glanced at his phone and did a double take. He had three missed calls, all from Euryale. What could have compelled her to reach out at this time of night? While they searched for clues to the source of the god killers, they'd kept their conversations otherwise neutral. At night, he went to his bed and she went to hers, and if he fantasized about what her body was like without clothes, that was between him and the single bathroom they shared.

"Still at the gym," he texted. "Is this an emergency?"

Her reply was swift. "No, I was just up and restless and wondered about American bars. Do you think we could go get a drink?"

Her inquiry was so unexpected that he stared at the phone. Lenno joined him and shot Asher a questioning glance that interrogated him without asking.

"You have the air of someone who's seen a Skinwalker."

"Seen a Gorgon," Asher said. "She wants to get a drink."

Lenno raised an eyebrow. "Almost the same thing. The devil you say. You said she didn't like to go out in public."

"I can't explain it." He showed Lenno the text. "Hell, she's a woman. They're always a mystery. I don't have the foggiest."

"I'd be curious to meet her. Want some company?"

* * *

She still waited for the hiss of her snakes when things grew quiet, and hadn't gotten used to the feel of the smoothness of skin instead of scales. Scales had their advantages, but she was enjoying the pliability of her new dermis. She didn't enjoy how it bruised and cut, though, and was still figuring out that she couldn't slam into things and expect that she wouldn't be damaged. She was immortal, not invulnerable.

She noticed the covert glances when she was out with Asher, the men who watched her as she walked past, those who cast admiring glances in her direction, hoping to catch her eye. It was a new sensation and not entirely welcome. On the rare occasions she caught her reflection, she had to force herself not to avert her eyes. In the past, even with her glamour in place, people perceived her differences on some level and shied away from her. Now humans were trying to get close. She wasn't in the habit of touching people and kept a safe distance. God forbid if she were to grow scales and snakes in the middle of a conversation.

In some ways that would be easier. She was a killing thing, designed to jump and howl and rend. She was a monster after all, though it no longer showed on the outside.

It had taken her a few days of examining her face and body to be sure that her human appearance had indeed stuck. It would be fitting for the Greek gods to restore her to her old form after giving her hope that she could live a normal life. It would be in Athena's foul, cruel nature to retract what she had done and return them to monsters. She knew better than to trust a god.

Asher and a man she didn't know had beaten her to the bar. She could have driven or hired a ride, but she still hadn't become comfortable with traffic and opted to walk. The streets were quieter than at rush hour, but even on a Wednesday, there was a fair number of cars on Sunset Boulevard. This city was so massive with its lights and sprawl and cars and people, that it made her want to shiver. She was not accustomed to the press of humanity.

When she entered the local bar, it was easy to spot the duo. The man who exhibited his heritage in his hair and skin, and who reeked of a combination of dragon and cat, was the first to notice her. He tapped Asher on the shoulder.

When Asher turned, her heart stopped. It wasn't just that he was striking, although he was, with his dark hair and fine build. This was Los Angeles, and she'd observed more gorgeous men in the last week than she could remember in eons. They couldn't hold their own next to the gods, of course, but some of the men and women in this vast city had demigod blood of their own. Like Asher. However, *unlike* Asher, many were using that to get ahead in the entertainment industry.

She studied the man with Asher. He had the taste of other, not god, but something more akin to what she was. It didn't surprise her that Asher hung around with his own kind. After all, he was both part monster, as banshees were considered, and part god.

"Elexis, this is Lenno. Before you ask, he's a Mishipeshu, a Native American water panther."

She reached over to shake Lenno's hand. "Nothing but gods and monsters here, eh?"

Lenno glanced around the bar, which was empty except for one man in the corner drinking. Then he shook Euryale's hand.

"Few more famous than you," he replied, and there was an edge to his voice. Euryale removed her hand, almost feeling his claws along her spine. The man didn't like her, that much was clear. The reason why was less apparent.

She nodded. "That is true. But it's my sister who is the legend, not me or Stheno. We Greeks have a thing about threes, in case you didn't notice. We were accessories after the fact."

"Were you?"

Her mouth twisted. She could fly to the ceiling, and with a cry that would shatter the glassware, come down on this presumptuous man and destroy every bone in his body. She didn't care what he was in his other form. It was of no concern how large he would be if he shifted. If he was to be insulting, they could have it out right now.

Lenno nodded. "I wasn't sure whether to believe the stories the gods fed Asher—they lie. You are what you say."

She scoffed. "You doubted it? Shall I prove it?" She barked a short noise that shook the glasses for no more than a second. The bartender turned, startled, and said, "earthquake" before the glasses and the man, settled back down again.

Lenno presented black fur and fangs, a giant form, more the size of a dragon than a panther, looming above him. She could see him in a split screen: man, and that massive dragon-like feline. She would have to study Mishipeshus when she had a moment. If Asher's friend was going to be a problem, she had to fix it now. If she had to take him out, she would want to do it sooner rather than later, after they'd gotten tied up in their quest.

"No need for that," Lenno said, raising his hands. "If the time comes when we must square off, then we will. For now, you and I are both friends of Asher's, and that's all that need be said."

She didn't want to back down. Her former self would have been taking chunks out of this presumptuous jerk. She was a Gorgon, and she bore the blood of gods. She could take a panther, no matter how big.

She should have gone with Asher to his gym. She would need to start burning off aggression.

"Deal," she said and held out her hand. Her instant dislike didn't burn away with the shaking of their palms, but it was a truce.

"What can I get ya?"

Asher lifted an eyebrow to Euryale and gestured to the bartender. "What's the woman's fancy?"

Her first drink after eons should be a momentous occasion. As a monster, she could not metabolize alcohol. Although some plants could get her stoned, she always needed to be alert. Today she could relax.

"I want…" she pondered, her gaze sweeping over the selection of bottles. "I want one of those drinks from the movies. With fruit and an umbrella and whipped cream, if you have it. Can you do something like that?"

Lenno laughed behind her and Asher drew in a breath. She turned to glare at him. "Girls are allowed to have fun, yes? Is this not a proper drink for a woman?"

Asher's face was dancing with amusement. "Absolutely."

"I can whip something up," the bartender said after a pause. "It'll be like a creamy sex on the beach, but I'll add fruit. That okay for the lady?"

The bartender was talking to Asher, and Euryale thought of protesting, but let it go.

Asher indicated to Euryale. "Better ask her. She gets irritated when she's disregarded."

"Right."

Euryale nodded. "That sounds fine." She'd lurked in caves for a long time, and some of those were near the water. She'd coupled with other monsters on the sand, but somehow it didn't have the same connotation as the images she retrieved from the bartender's mind. He'd had sex on the beach, and found it fun, but wet and sandy. Still, the woman who he'd been with gave the best blow jobs…Euryale was caught in the memory of a mouth on her cock, suckling. Desire speared through her in a wave, one not her own.

Asher shook her and she met his gaze.

"I felt it, too," he said, jerking his chin at the man, now focused on making the drink. There was something almost plaintive about the bartender's memory, a love gone perhaps, or the loss of a talented sex partner.

Lenno drummed his fingers on the bar while Asher and Euryale studied each other. Something primal crawled up her spine, a reaction more in line with her previous self than today's person. This form wouldn't just grab a man and throw him to the floor and ride him. Yet the bartender's intense memory flooded Euryale with that desire. She craved fulfilling the ache that swept through her like a firestorm, leaving her body shaking and her nerve endings alive with sensation.

"It was different when I was a mon…when I was away from others." She couldn't say that her abilities as a monster didn't always permit the ability to hear others. It was iffy in that form, and inconsistent. Now, as a goddess, it was all around her. Another reason to stay away from people. "I'm not used to being in such close company. It must happen from time to time." This had been a mistake. Her other self could go to the woods and let off steam. She could use her snakes to paralyze and eat victims. She had done all those things and more. Desire throbbed between her legs, making her irritable.

"You'll grow accustomed to it. We'll get a drink and have some fun."

"Yes," she agreed. "Let's do that."

* * *

The Uber deposited the two of them in front of Asher's house and took off into the night. Euryale stumbled out of the back seat and almost tripped over the broken sidewalk. Asher followed, though not in much better shape than she was. It was after two, they'd stayed at the bar until it closed, but Lenno had left after one beer. They would have to discuss the dislike that was palpable between the two of them, but that was a problem for another day. Tonight, he'd done what Euryale asked and that was to have a drink, or three or four, and a good time. There was something different about her, something that made his body stand up and notice her curves.

The fact that she was reserved was fine. But it was more than that. Asher sighed, and stuck the house key into the lock. He shouldn't be trying to figure out what it was about Euryale that called to him. He should be running for the hills.

She was, at the end, still a Gorgon. Even if she didn't have snakes for hair, she was still a monster. Danger lurked from more than one corner, and none so dangerous as the woman in his spare bedroom.

"That drink was so sweet," she said. "I don't know how I managed it."

"You managed three of them," Asher replied, tossing his keys on a nearby table and kicking off his shoes. They clattered on the hardwood and Euryale followed suit. She was tall enough not to need heels, but he imagined even if she were five feet tall, this woman wouldn't wear lifts. It would get in the way if she had to fight.

"I did, didn't I?" she said and there was distinct mirth on her face. "That was fun, Asher. Thank you for meeting me. Even if your friend was a bore."

"He's careful around new people," Asher said. His friend's intense dislike had taken Asher by surprise. He had to remember that the Gorgons were not well-liked. They'd done a lot of things that would be hard to put aside, but they hadn't asked to be turned into monsters. It was no different than Lenno in his other form, or Asher when the banshee took over. He would have to remind Lenno of that fact when they met again. Whatever it took, this was a task he had to fulfill, and he'd been assigned to work with the Gorgon. He could not fail. He was all too aware of the price if he did. The gods, they didn't take failure well. He had a sword looming over his head.

She peeked up at him beneath her lashes, and there was mischief dancing across her face, a sparkle that made him want to lean over and kiss her, taste that mouth for himself. He took a step closer to her, about to act on his impulse. Euryale stood there watching him. His pulse sped up at the idea of touching her. His fingers curled against his palms and he moved toward her, ready to grip her shoulders and put his mouth on hers.

A mental blast shot across his senses. Euryale winced. Asher closed the distance between them and hauled her into the shadows. If this person was about to break into his house, it was best not to be so conspicuous.

The thrust came again, and his temples pounded with pain from the assault. He detected Euryale strengthening her shields, but they were both slow from the alcohol. He cursed the fact that he'd had one too many. He should've known better. He must always be on guard.

"Whoever it is, I don't think they are familiar with who they're pursuing," Euryale whispered, her words less slurred than they were a moment ago. He could almost feel the alcohol leaving her system. He didn't have the same power.

"Why do you think that?" he asked, wishing the living room light wasn't on. It was too bright in the room, and their shadows would be spotted. His weapon of choice, a less-than-legal knife, he'd left in his bedroom when he'd gone to the gym. Dumb, dumb, dumb. He had a firearm, but it was locked away in the gun safe. He hadn't trusted himself to leave it out with Euryale in the house. Foolish. So foolish.

The mental strike came again. It had a diffuse quality to it; for all its power, something that was more like the scattershot of a rifle than the precision of a sniper. Maybe Euryale was right.

His head ached like he had a migraine. He could feel something probing, trying to find their quarry.

The mind had a quality that he'd only experienced when dealing with a god. He was familiar with the feeling. There were a lot of gods and demigods in this city. He hadn't dealt with the Queen of the Banshees, Clíodhna, in some time, but he'd never forgotten the strength of her psyche.

"I sense a god," he said, sliding down against the wall. If something was going to come through the door or window, they would be facing it when it happened.

"Me too. This is a fishing expedition, Asher. It is similar to many a time when gods or heroes went in search of us to try and prove their worth to their pantheon."

He shot her an amused glance, wishing alcohol wasn't still coursing through his system. There was something so matter-of-fact about the way she said it.

"And did they?"

Her gaze was focused on the front door. "Besides Perseus, how many tales have you read of people beating the Gorgons?"

"That's a no, then."

"That's a no."

Little warriors, little warriors, where are you? Little warriors, come out and play. I know you're out there. Do not think you can win this game. I outmatch you.

Asher tasted the feel of the god's mind on his tongue, but once again, Euryale was quicker.

"It's female. I can't tell what pantheon. She's too well shielded to trace her power back to its source, but it has the flavor of a woman. It's a goddess and not a minor one."

Asher frowned. "A god? Could they be taking down their own?"

There was a rustling outside and they both went still. When the sound came again, just the flutter of leaves and creak of shingles, he let out a breath. Just the wind. Damn it, he wished he weren't drunk. His thoughts were muddy, his reflexes slow. If someone came for them right now, he wouldn't be able to fight with his usual ability.

Euryale fixed her attention on the yard beyond his front door and appeared to be listening. After several moments she also relaxed. "It's weather and perhaps a night predator. Maybe a raccoon. We had those in Wyoming. They are nocturnal."

"Yeah. Sometimes they're under my house at three in the morning. Pests."

"As to your question, I'm not sure. You haven't been around a lot of gods, correct?"

He nodded. "Ares, of course. There are many gods in Los Angeles, but few from a major pantheon. Clíodhna, but not since I moved here."

"I have dealt with the Greeks, and some of the others who most humans are unfamiliar with. Those gods have a power to their mental signature that is unmistakable. This doesn't feel quite like a major goddess such as Athena, *curse her*, but it's a force to be reckoned with. My guess would be a god one step below the big ones."

"And you think this is the one who's been killing gods?"

"Or at least the power behind it. I doubt she's doing the dirty work."

"Great."

Chapter Four

Little warriors, you cannot fight me.

Euryale focused on the mental voice. All vestiges of alcohol fled her system. She reached out and found voices all around her, competing for her attention. The questing signature was out there somewhere, but it was too muddied with all the other input to find the one that was trying to track them. What was working in her and Asher's favor was also helping the other. She poked around for a few minutes but came up empty.

"We could let her find us and trace it back." Asher's suggestion was half-hearted, and she gave him an incredulous glare.

"No thanks. So far, we have the element of surprise. If we give that up before we learn more, we lose any advantage we have."

He shook his head like a dog, and she had a flash moment of awareness of the world gone fuzzy. Asher was still drunk. There had been a moment where she believed he was going to kiss her. She would have let him. She sought to taste his full lips. But there was little time for that.

Too bad.

"Damn it, you're right. What's the plan?"

She rose from their crouched position and Asher followed.

"If the goddess is searching for us on the mental plane, then she doesn't know who or where we are. She's hoping we're dumb enough to make a mistake. I don't think she expects to find us, but she can try. She senses that we're out there, so someone tipped her off to our quest."

He frowned, and she had to fight not to reach over and smooth those lines out of his forehead. He appeared twenty-five years old, although he had said he was a hundred. Just a baby, to her. A hundred years was nothing to a creature who had lived since before the current calendar. Damn the gods, anyway. He was an attractive specimen in any culture, and able to wreak havoc with her libido.

Little warriors, come out and play.

The mental voice was further away now, the goddess apparently close to giving up her quest.

"She will stop soon. She wanted us to understand she's aware we were out there. On the off chance she got lucky, she gave it a try."

He shook his head and then stumbled a little. "Got it. No more drinking for the duration of this little party. I can't afford to be muzzy again. We were lucky tonight. That's a neat trick you've got there to stop being drunk. Can you teach me?"

"I didn't realize I could still do it."

He stumbled and nearly fell before he recovered himself. "What do you mean?"

Euryale moved away from him and went to the front door to finish securing it. Then she turned off the living room light and flipped on a table lamp.

"They restored some, but not all of my abilities. I must find out what I have to work with. They took away my ability to turn men to stone, but that was more my sister's gift. I don't have my protective scales, but I can be wounded. There are many things I can do that I have to become familiar with again. Functions I could perform in my original form were useless to me as a monster. I am a goddess. We have talents other than what is written about in books."

He gave her a quick glance and then ran his hands through his hair. "Maybe I've got stuff buried in my heritage that will help me, too. I should go to bed and sober up for morning. We need to start our mission in earnest. Are you ready?"

The perverse part of her wished for him to return to her and finish what had been on his mind before the goddess interrupted, but that was a stupid thing to want. They were partners, and when they had solved the mystery, they would go their separate ways. She was a Gorgon, after all, and had spent eons as a beast. A youngling like Asher had other things to occupy his time than a monster from legend. She had to remember that and not get lost in the promise of his gaze.

* * *

Asher groaned when he rolled out of bed the next morning. His head pounded and it wasn't all from drinking. The invasion of the deity, whoever or whatever she was, left a lingering effect on his body. He scratched his chest and then contemplated the day. By the chirp of the birds and the angle of the sun, he guessed it was around seven a.m. Early for him.

He had two text messages from his agent, no doubt new booking opportunities. Asher groaned at the hit his career would take while he was off on this jaunt. You were hot one day and gone the next—easily forgotten. Voiceover work was better than most, but still, he was taking a big risk by abandoning his career just when it was getting hot.

"There's coffee if you need some."

Euryale's voice was far too cheerful for this time of day. He shrugged into a T-shirt and ran his fingers through his hair before venturing into the living room. Now he could smell the scent of the beans permeating the air. Although he had a single-brew pot, Euryale tended to use the other one. He wouldn't have imagined a Gorgon drinking coffee, but there were many things he didn't know about Euryale. Like the way she would feel under him, kissing him.

Asher cut off that line of thinking before it could become embarrassing under his loose sweats. She may appear human, but she wasn't, and he had no idea what she was thinking. They had a job to do and having sex with the Gorgon wasn't in the description.

"I did a little digging while you were sleeping," she said and flipped over a tablet.

He cocked an eyebrow. She was also wearing sleep clothes: in her case, a shirt and a pair of plaid shorts. The shorts didn't display her thighs, they were baggy, but her calves were visible. Gorgons shaved or didn't have hair at all. He suspected the former as the Greeks were born in a time before razors were popular. So many things and so many centuries to account for. He couldn't even imagine living that long. He would outlive all his current human friends, and the next batch after that. And after that. But it was nothing compared to a goddess.

"How long have you been awake?"

Euryale's body was stiff, at odds with her languid pose. "I don't sleep much. I was nocturnal before, but I'm still adjusting to the new form. I started checking for anomalies and oddities to narrow down who we are searching for."

He sipped the coffee, which was decent enough, and pointed with his free hand to the screen.

"Smart. What did you find? Anything interesting?"

She sat cross-legged on the floor and the action made the shorts slide up her thigh. Asher coveted following the dark shadows all the way up to her cleft, where she was soft, and maybe wet. There was something seductive in the way she moved, but that might be his fevered imagination.

"If you follow their path, which was no easy feat, let me tell you, the trail starts with those pantheons so old that they are remembered by, at best, a handful of people."

He nodded. "We've already been over this. I told you."

"Right. Sorry. I'm gathering information so some of what I am saying may be repetition."

"No need to apologize. I'm still feeling the effects of last night. I should be apologizing."

"Accepted. Thank you. Here's what I have so far."

She spread out torn pages from a spiral notebook he'd forgotten he owned. He glanced at them. Her handwriting was awful, almost impossible to read.

"You're going to have to decipher this. What language did you write it in?"

She shook her head and tapped one of the pages. "English, you idiot, but I'm not used to holding a pen. In the past, even when my form seemed human, I had scales and claws. It made writing and using a computer difficult. They called me the 'granola woman' in Wyoming for a reason. Hippies can eschew technology in a way few others can get away with. Get another cup of coffee, and then I'll explain."

He wondered how she'd lived all those millennia. He would bet there was more than just the Greek legends. Perhaps others had been inspired by them, just as there had been tales inspired by his clan. They weren't so far apart, his mother's family and the Gorgons, although he doubted Euryale would want to hear that.

When he returned, she thrust a paper at him. It listed many names he recognized, and others that he didn't. He frowned and sipped his second cup of coffee, letting the heat and taste of the brew flow through him to clear his head. No more drinking, at least not until this mission was over. Then he might get good and drunk, if he survived. He might be immortal or simply long-lived. Banshees died, gods did not, and he had yet to discern which bloodline was stronger. As he showed no sign of aging, and those banshees he was raised with were starting to age, he thought the latter.

"You did what with the search engines, now?" He studied the first name. "Echo?"

She smoothed the pages and made some notes on a fresh piece.

"I searched for myths and legends surrounding those with powers similar to ours. The gods didn't just lift my curse because they liked me. They need us, and there has to be a connection."

"Don't you think if they grasped who was doing this, they would go after them themselves?"

"Maybe. Maybe not. Maybe they don't want to make it easy for us. I believe they don't know who is responsible for this, or they would have tried to get Zeus to smite her. Then again, Zeus also doesn't do what people want, not even his pantheon. Unless it involves a woman. What do you remember about Echo?"

"Shit, you would ask me that. Um…" He searched his memory. "Echo was a mountain nymph who consorted with Zeus and earned Hera's wrath. As punishment for playing with her husband, Hera made it impossible for Echo to do anything other than repeat a person's last words back to them. She would have reason to hate the Greek gods. If we're going with the assumption that we're trying to find a woman, and a goddess with aural power, then I agree Echo would be on the list," he said. "But is she alive?"

Euryale pursed her lips, and Asher felt a sense of desire pulsing from her, or maybe he was imagining it. "I don't know," she admitted. "It's possible with a background like that, that a, pardon the pun, echo of her remains. There are rumors she bore Pan children, despite her lack of interest in him. The Greeks were not picky about forcing their attention on unwilling maidens. It's conceivable she may yet live. Or her children took up her cause. She's a suspect."

"That makes sense." He peered at the next name. "I'm unfamiliar with this one."

"Homados. He's Greek and is the god of battle-noise. It fits. He's part of the Machai, the spirits of battle and combat. They are the sons and daughters of Eris. He would have the power, but perhaps not the desire. They operate as a group, those Machai, and he is only one of many. Not all are sonically gifted."

"Maybe he thought it was time to go out on his own," Asher mused. "In all these centuries, this Homados guy took a chance to cut loose from the crew. I think that they are potentials. What else?"

"This one may be a long shot, but I didn't want to exclude him."

Asher frowned. "Enlil? From the saga of Gilgamesh? From what little I remember, all he did was complain about noise. He didn't have that sort of power. Isn't he Babylonian, or something? Talk about forgotten."

"Sumerian. Yes, he complained, and the gods destroyed mankind because of it. Perhaps he feels he has been demonized in the saga and decided to seek revenge."

Asher shook his head, taking another sip of coffee. "That's a stretch. Besides, he's a guy."

"Agreed, but I'm covering all possibilities."

"Okay. Who's this one?"

She checked her notes on the paper. "Anat. Caananite goddess of war and strife. Could have a sound component to it."

He tried to keep his face neutral. "You covered all the bases."

She put down her pen. "You're laughing at me."

"Who's this?" he asked to forestall the storm gathering in her dour expression.

"That's Tlaloc. Aztec god of rain and thunder, and more I am not sure about."

Asher frowned. "He would fit the profile, but what reason would he have for going after the other gods? He's a major god himself. I think the person or people have to be those who feel disenfranchised. We should keep to the minor gods and, or, pantheons, or immortals. We'll find our perpetrators there.

"Perhaps Tlaloc wants to take over."

He grimaced. "If he did, he's far too late. People remember the Aztec gods as ancient bloodthirsty beings. They don't have the myths and legends that the Greeks, Romans, Egyptians, and the Norse do. He can kill as many as he likes, and the Aztecs still won't come to prominence. Besides, we heard a woman last night."

"Perhaps his companion."

Asher shook his head. "Euryale, this is good stuff, but we shouldn't be wasting time on dead ends. Can I ask you a question?"

"Sure."

"What made the gods so sure it wasn't you and your sisters doing this? Why did they turn to you for help instead of thinking you were the culprits?"

* * *

Euryale observed him for several moments, absorbing his words. The beast that still lurked inside her, contemplated leaping on him and rending him with her claws. She flexed her hands, almost feeling his flesh tear, before remembering that she had fingers, and not weapons at the end of her hand.

"Is that what you think? Or what you are wondering? If the Gorgons are responsible for this?"

Asher looked away, his discomfort visible in every line of his body. Good.

He may be a banshee, but her voice could hold her own with his, or better. She had the advantage. She could shatter him. She could jump with him to a high mountain and drop him off…She could…

He was staring at her, the line of his cock visible against his shorts. He must have caught—or intuited—what she'd been thinking. Last night there had been a moment when she was sure he was going to kiss her. The female part of her would have welcomed that touch. Now that was out the window. Like everyone else, he only identified Gorgons with monsters, and not the goddesses they had been before the transformation. No surprise. She sighed and shook her hands, losing the sensation of claws. "You're right, Asher. We would have been under suspicion if the gods weren't able to pinpoint all the Gorgons. The three of us together are a powerful force, but Medusa is in stasis, Saskia is in the Middle East, and I was in Wyoming. I'm sure they checked on our whereabouts before offering me the deal."

He frowned. "You're the descendants of gods. You must have other powers."

"Not to get through Earth and back in the span of a night. That is saved for earth talents and the Elementals. Not me. I have no doubt the last time a god was killed, Athena had us investigated. At some point they came to the conclusion that we could be useful. It's how they work."

His pause was lengthy. "Did it occur to you that by offering to take away your curse and giving you a human appearance, they diminished your controls? Your claws and scales made you a weapon. Turning men to stone made all fear you. Why not leave you a monster if they were sure you weren't the perpetrator?"

She wasn't used to using her mouth for emotions other than snarling. Now she let a faint air of scorn cross her countenance while tilting up her lips.

"I had no incentive to help them if they left me as I was. Humanity was that lure. Yes, it restored what they had taken away, but they, alone, had the power to do that. I did them no good as a beast. I believe they also worried I could join the other forces."

"Would you have?"

She paused to consider. "I might have. I have no love for the gods. This is expedience. I'm tired of hiding in this world. Just because the glamour shows me as a human doesn't mean I am. I was sick of pretending. Now I can interact as others do. It's not enough to make up for millennia of being punished, but I can't change what came before. I can only do what is in front of me now."

He nodded, and she detected a faint approval in his mind. "I accept your answer. It wasn't a fair question to ask. Back to the task at hand. You did some good research. I think the next step is to go to Europe. Do you have a passport?"

Chapter Five

"Asher, how long are we going to be traveling?"

Euryale eyed the pile of stuff in his bedroom and raised an eyebrow at the man. He had an aura of smugness, rocking back on his heels in satisfaction, if his mental signature was any indication.

"As long as we need to."

She glanced at her suitcase and back at him. "It's supposed to be women who pack too much stuff."

She had no idea what was going on inside his head. All she could pick up was the earlier sense of self-assuredness.

"First, we're off to Ireland to visit my mother and the banshees. Then we're going to go to Albania to talk to the pantheon. Then we may travel to the remains of the Guanches, but their loss was further back. They may not have much to offer us by way of clues. We might be able to skip that country. I need a lot of stuff." His gaze moved from his suitcase and then to the woman in the doorway. She wished she knew what he was thinking, but he gave her no clues. "Before long, we have to go to Greece. It only makes sense."

Euryale took a step back and glanced at the bed, the suitcase, and then a spot above his head.

"Ugh." She made a face, pulling her cheeks down. "You're right, but I don't want to. That wretched goddess is there."

The superior feeling faded from his mind. Now she could sense anxiety behind it, the conceit a mask.

"We don't have a choice. People choose what they're most familiar with. These murderers, whoever they are, have targeted other pantheons, but I can't shake the feeling that Greece and the Greek gods are their endgame. Therefore, it needs to be ours."

"I am aware. I'll do what I have to do, however reluctantly."

He eyed her for a long time, saying nothing. "There's more than reluctance," he said and stepped toward her. Euryale didn't move from her position in the doorway, but all her muscles tensed to flee. "I understand that you don't want to, but that's not it. You're scared to go back to your home country, isn't that right?"

She scoffed, trying for disdainful, but afraid she had only managed pathetic. "Just because I no longer have the appearance of a monster doesn't mean that I'm not still considered one. There are plenty of those who would love to take my head, just to say that they took the head of a Gorgon."

"And that frightens you?" His lifted eyebrow—*drat that piece of his anatomy*—told her she'd disappointed him.

She stood straight and raised her chin. "Of course not. The Greeks don't concern me. I am still more powerful than most. I spent a lot of years in caves in the hills outside Athens, before I started exploring this big world of ours. I don't want to go back there until I have to."

"We have to. First, we're going to Ireland to meet my mother, as well as talk to the Queen of the Banshees."

A vision of a grey-and-russet-haired woman with a semi-lined face flowed into her mind. She couldn't detect the resemblance, but maybe that was to be expected when a race wasn't supposed to produce male children.

"Why are we going to the banshees? Do they have something to add to this search?"

His eyebrows drew together. A low-level thrum of desire still pulsed within her, reminding her again that the banshee had almost kissed her. And oh, she'd coveted that kiss. Tenderness was not a tenet of her everyday life as a Gorgon. She hadn't realized she'd missed it. The only time they had that kind of emotion was when the sisters were around each other, and that hadn't happened in decades.

She shouldn't want it now. It was idiocy.

"It's Clíodhna's prerogative as Queen. Also, Mother wants to meet you. Besides, it sounds like one of the Tuatha dé Danann was taken out by this group."

Euryale whistled. Another pantheon. Another goddess. Asher had been raised by women, and he didn't have the anathema for them that she did. Still, she had shown reluctance once and she wasn't about to show it again. Emotion was weakness.

"If you say so. I am aware of the pantheon in Ireland, but I forget your queen's name. What is it again?"

"Clíodhna. She's a member of the Tuatha dé Danann. There are many legends about her, just as there are about all gods and goddesses. The Irish are a poetic bunch and the stories are fanciful. She is our queen and deserves my respect and fealty, but she also has a tale to relay. Therefore, our first stop is Ireland. County Cork to be exact, a place called Mallow."

"It's a waste of time. We should be hunting god killers, not meeting vain queens of tribes of women."

His gaze was speculative when he considered her. That near kiss danced across her memory, the possibility of being touched searing her. A fluttering stirred in her belly that wasn't quite desire, it was too subtle an emotion for that. It was something else, an unfamiliar feeling both transient and elusive. She wasn't sure she liked it.

"She has knowledge of this killer. Euryale, you're a goddess and you should remember that. You've forgotten that the blood of gods run in your veins. Not just half god, like me, yours is pure. You're named in myths, whereas I'll never be in stories. Did it ever occur to you that these god killers could turn their attention to you?"

* * *

She was a stubborn one.

Asher watched Euryale as they flew across the continent on their way to his family in Ireland. He could feel her reluctance to meet the banshees, but after her initial outburst, said nothing further.

What she did do, to his frustration, was lapse into the kind of silence that even a woman who was a former beast used to telegraph her unhappiness. She may have once shredded someone who offended her with her claws, but her quiet achieved the same goal.

He'd offered to spring for first class, but Euryale wouldn't hear of it. She insisted on sitting in coach, just like she had on those rare occasions when she'd flown. He would have loved to have pampered her with the experience, but she refused. Now she was in the middle seat of the plane, squished between him and a slender young woman. He would've traded with her, but she didn't want that, either.

She was so stubborn, it made his teeth clench.

She was faced out the window, watching the scenery go by on this bright, cloudless day. The vistas fascinated her, and he wondered what she was thinking. Not that she would tell him. Her mind was closed and barred.

"When we get to New York, we're going to have a few hours before we go to Ireland. Is there anything you want to do?"

Euryale turned her attention to him, but her thoughts seemed far away. He pondered whether she'd been communing with the birds. He had no knowledge of how it worked with monsters. Maybe they had a special talent with animals that he didn't have. There could be shifters among the birds—or he was overthinking the entire thing.

Then she flashed him a quick grin. "No," she said after some consideration. "It's all a bit much. This"—She gestured with the arm nearest him to indicate the plane—"this reminds me I'm not used to a lot of people. I think that giant city may be more than I can handle right now. I stayed away from cities for a"—She shook herself and modified whatever she'd been about to say—"For a long time."

He hoped his sigh of relief wasn't audible. He gestured to his phone. "I've got wi-fi on the plane. Want me to switch to first class for the flight over? It might not be too late."

He waited, wondering why he cared. These new feelings were unexpected, and unwelcome. His friend didn't like her, and for good reason, and he shouldn't like her, either. But he did.

He sensed a thread of anxiety under her shield. The press of humanity had been a test; one she didn't think she had passed.

"I get it. Planes suck no matter how you cut it. It was brave of you to want to fly coach, but we can at least get business class if there's room. You don't have to squish yourself into an inadequate seat. I've got the money…"

"I don't," she said, her gaze darting away from him.

"They're paying us well, and I'll make sure they compensate us for the flights. No need to worry."

You're going to make a god pay your travel expenses?

Our travel expenses, and yes.

He breathed out a sigh of relief that she was speaking to him.

"Okay, whatever you say, ban…Asher."

Her eyes were troubled. In the week she'd been at his house, she had kept to the twilight and early dawn hours, and spent much of the time in the house during the day. As a monster, even a cloaked one, it was easier to move in the night. There was no getting around the fact that she was a ruthless killer.

His body stirred, reminding him that whatever she was, she was also an alluring woman who called to him on a level he hadn't experienced in a long time.

"When we get to JFK, we'll go to the lounge and wait. I would like to show you New York sometime. It's a city that must be experienced."

Now her gaze was amused.

"Asher, I've seen things you cannot imagine, cities you will never witness. Ones that are now ruins under the water, or in rubble under the ground. New York is just another place. Man puts far too much stock in their skyscrapers."

With that, she leaned back and said nothing further, leaving him non-plussed as well as one-upped.

* * *

Ireland was a country she hadn't spent much time in in centuries, but she was familiar with its rolling green hills. It was full of shadows and blood, its history as intense as anything the Greeks had to offer. She was aware of the Tuatha dé Danann and the Fomorians, as well as some of the other Irish gods who inhabited this land. Clíodhna was one of their main goddesses, as well as being Queen of the Banshees. Euryale had spent centuries staying away from people, and now she was in the company of this attractive man. As a monster, she'd taken what she craved when carnal desire had come over her, but as a goddess, she was more circumspect. It was folly to get involved with a man like Asher. It could only lead to disaster.

They landed in Cork, a city she hadn't visited since it had been little more than a battleground for the Vikings in the ninth century. That had been a wild time, and the ferocity of those early settlers suited her. She was fond of the green hills, but the gods weren't too happy with a Gorgon in their midst, so Euryale had moved on.

Asher glanced at her when they arrived at the car. She had spent the better part of the last decades in America and was more used to driving on the right side of the road. She went to get in on the side nearest the curb, but that was where the driver's side was.

Asher gave her an amused glance. "Do you want to drive?"

She pondered the vehicle and then shook her head.

He opened the passenger door, ushering her in before the cars bore down on them. Although she had once made her home in England, it had been before cars existed.

The trip to Mallow was around forty-three kilometers from the airport. Asher had rented them a room at a hotel in the center of the town where they were now heading.

"You'll be able to do whatever you want to, once this is over," Asher said. By the expression on his face it wasn't anything close to what he had been about to say.

"I'm still getting used to being able to move freely in the world. It's going to take more than a few weeks for me to adjust. I can't decide anything until our mission is done. If we fail, Athena will have no compunction about turning me and my sisters back into monsters. It's not smart to plan too far in advance."

To her surprise, Asher's hands curled into fists and his brows drew together until they were almost one thing.

"I'm not going to let that happen," he said, and the words held the ring of a vow.

Even though it wasn't polite, Euryale laughed. "How are you going to stop it? Athena is one of the great goddesses of the pantheon, and you are a demigod. You have little chance of winning her over."

Asher opened his mouth to say something but shook his head and turned his attention to the road. Euryale watched the scenery while Asher pointed out interesting tidbits. She could have checked the sights on her phone but enjoyed discovering things without the aid of modern technology.

They parked in front of an inn at the end of a driveway. It appeared more like a castle with its grey stone and turret, but Asher had been assured this was an inn. There were paranormal beings here, the air was thick with them. She could feel that this area was the home to the Queen of the Banshees, and many others of her kind as well. Euryale could hear whispers of the Tuatha dé Danann, and a hint of fairies and sprites around them. Ireland had many supernatural creatures lurking in the bogs and woods. The old lands housed many interesting beings, which was why she'd gone to America. That land had its share, but few were native to the land. Only those like Lenno, and the Native American gods could call America home. The others were transplants. In addition, the hustle and bustle of the Americans kept them to a minimum.

Asher emerged from the driver's side and motioned for Euryale to go inside. She ducked under the vine-covered entryway to enter a foyer with a red-faced woman on the other side of the counter. The woman's attention was fixed on Euryale's face.

Asher was entering with their luggage, when the woman released a wail. She opened her mouth wide and howled, pointing at Euryale at the same time.

Chapter Six

"Stop yer screeching," a voice said from the other side of the room. A moment later another woman entered, this one taller than the still-howling woman. She gave the clerk an impatient glare and shoved her with her elbow.

"Cop on, Miriam, don't be acting the muppet just because you are in the presence of a Gorgon. There are monsters everywhere. She is a fine thing now, not gacky-looking anymore. Quit yer squealing or I'll shut yer mouth for you, like."

The woman Asher assumed was Miriam closed her mouth on that last statement, cutting off her scream mid-howl. As he watched, some of the redness faded from her face. Her hair, an orange-red color that he doubted was the color she was born with, showed a flush at its roots. Tears glistened as she backed away from the counter, her gaze fixed on Euryale.

There was a crumpled quality to Euryale's face, a brittle air of pain and regret. It made Asher want to shove the woman named Miriam out the door before she could hurt Euryale further. He turned to the new woman.

"Get her out of here. She's scaring my friend."

The other woman, a stout middle-aged matron, scoffed loud and smoothed back her hair.

"Dry your arse, son of Roisin. We don't like Greek monsters here, but at least she's not a Fomorian. Go on with you, Miriam. Go sweep the kitchen or something. Make yerself useful. I'll tend to these two."

The inn they'd booked had been a recommendation through his mother, and Asher had no doubt the banshee network was in full swing. What was odd to him was that they hadn't expected Euryale. They'd been told two were coming to speak to Clíodhna. Perhaps Roisin supposed the pair wouldn't be welcome at the inn if they'd been alerted to expect one of the immortal Gorgons. She could have helped facilitate the introduction, if she'd been at the inn when he arrived. He glanced around, wondering if he'd missed her.

"Where is my mother? She's supposed to be here."

"She's legging it as we speak. Mind yerself, like. She will be here before the sun goes down."

He crossed his arms, wanting to find his mother right now and talk to her. He had a feeling this was some sort of test. He didn't like it. Not at all.

"She should be here. We came all this way."

"Lad, you need to learn patience." Her attention fixed on Euryale, and for a moment, Asher detected respect in the woman's gaze. "As I am sure the Gorgon here has after so many centuries."

There was little response to that, and Asher was relieved that Euryale offered none. She stood rooted in place, her interest on a lattice outside the window twined with purple flowers.

"If she isn't welcome here, we can go to another inn. Where Euryale goes, I go. We're not only here to see my mother, but also your queen…"

The woman cut Asher off. "Your queen, too, my lad. You're her subject as well, for all that you are part god." Her sniff showed that she didn't care much for the gods. This whole thing was less and less to Asher's liking. He considered scooping Euryale up and taking her away from Mallow County. Screw the meeting with Clíodhna. Euryale didn't deserve to be treated like a second-class citizen.

Some of what he was thinking must have shown on Asher's face because the yet-to-be-named woman sighed and nodded at Euryale.

"I'm talking blarney. I'm forgetting my manners, I am. You are a guest in our country, and even though we have no truck with Greeks, you have done nothing to us. For Roisin's sake, you are also welcome." She gave Euryale an appraising stare, her gaze sweeping from the top of Euryale's curly brown hair to her sneaker-clad feet. "You are calling yourself Elexis, although your name is Euryale. The 'far roaming' one. You are aptly named to visit our shores. The banshees welcome you."

Euryale opened and shut her mouth, glancing at Asher for confirmation of what to say. But he was at as big a loss as she was.

"Thank you, um…"

"Nuala. You didn't think we would house you anywhere but with the banshees, did you? Will you be wanting one room or two? We have you down for two, but I don't like to make assumptions."

Asher had spent many nights in the house with Euryale, but his body burned with the idea of being alone with her in a hotel room. He glanced at the Gorgon, who was frowning.

His libido deflated. Although his blood heated with the idea of being alone with her in such close proximity, it didn't appear to appeal to Euryale. Too bad. It could have been fun.

"Two is perfect, Nuala." He laid down his platinum credit card. "If you've got suites, that would be great."

Nuala snorted. "Look around you, son of Roisin. This is a castle, not some modern building for you to go fannying about. Does it appear we have suites for the asking? We are not the Ritz or the Four Seasons, if you be wanting that, you are in the wrong place."

Euryale still had that frown line between her brows, and Asher had an urge to kiss it away. She was such a prickly thing, quick to lash out. It would take a while for her reactions of a millennium to fade. He would have to be patient.

"Two rooms, then, Nuala. Best you've got. Elexis is still getting used to it all."

The banshee cast Euryale a glance. Asher recognized he'd said a dumb thing. Again. He was making a habit of stupid statements around her, like a kid who just met a glamorous movie star and was twisted up inside. He didn't have any idea what to say or do.

"They're all the same, but I'll give you the ones with the best view. They've got a door connecting them if you be wanting to talk in the late night. That's the closest we get to a fancy hotel." Her twinkling blue eyes suggested she might be laughing at him, but Asher was too off-kilter to respond to her banter.

"That will do, thank you." He yearned to take the shadows away from Euryale and replace them with delight. This Gorgon had somehow slid inside his defenses and made him want things from her he had no business wanting. She was hundreds of years older than him, *and* a goddess. He was in every way a child to her more mature person, even with their disparity in height and apparent strength.

"Asher?"

He tried but failed to get a smile to come to his lips. He gestured to where the clerk was processing his card.

"Like I said before, I have plenty of money. I'm a sought-after voiceover artist and never lack for work. I specialize in sounds nobody else, not even a machine can make. You don't need to worry about money. Besides, we've got the credit balance from the gods, remember? We can use that if you're not sure about taking money from me."

Nuala clicked her tongue. "You shouldn't be using your talent that way, young banshee. It isn't done, like."

In any other situation he would be mad at Nuala for her interference, but he could have kissed her for distracting Euryale. It was a funny thing to think she was worried about his finances. Few others had ever been concerned about whether or not he could pay the bills. More often than not, the women he'd encountered were willing to let him pay for the pleasure of their company.

"These are new times, Nuala. There are new ways of doing things. Not all of us are with the gods in Ireland, away from the day-to-day reality of humans. We have to adapt."

Even as he said it, he wondered if Euryale could adjust to this era, or if she would always be stuck in the old. Her life had been as a monster for longer than he could imagine, and while she was adjusting well, that other side could surface at any time. He wasn't sure she could ever be comfortable living as a human.

There was no reason why he should be wondering what her body would be like on the beds of this inn, stretched out naked and waiting for him on the covers.

* * *

She didn't like Ireland. She didn't want to be here.

Euryale paced in the room they had been provided, staring at the closed door that separated their spaces. She considered knocking but, in the end, did not. It was early but she was awake, thrown off by the time change and the travel and… just everything. Asher was shut down to her but something new lurked behind his mind. She couldn't help but wonder what it was.

Before, when she'd been a goddess, she was fierce and not shy. It was harder than she had estimated being part of humanity again. It had been easier being a monster. At least then she understood what was expected of her.

She missed being in Asher's home, the casual intimacy they had shared in mornings or late nights, the sound of him showering or puttering around in the other room.

Deciding against knocking, she changed into sweats to go for a run. She'd burn off some of this excess energy and put it to good use.

To her surprise, Asher was outside stretching. The sweat on his sleeveless grey top and damp hair indicated that he had already finished exercising. He raised a hand in greeting and rose to his full height. He was appealing in the Irish dawn, with their sleep schedules turned upside down, and his dark hair and one-day beard glinting in the early sun. The sweat and salt of his skin would taste good if she licked it off.

Damn it. She was attracted to him. The surge in her belly and the warmth that flowed through her made a mockery of any denial. Here in the green-and-mist-covered morning, she understood that she had been aware of him as a woman is to a man since almost the beginning. She wanted to flee from it, and, also lean in closer, breathe in the musky scent of him and feel his well-muscled arms before she kissed those full lips. It was too much and she needed to run away, and also to stay.

He grinned at her and shoved a hand through his hair, sending his untidy locks into spikes from the damp. From the sweat darkening his clothes, he had been jogging for a while. She wasn't sure how she missed him leaving the inn, but, somehow, she must have.

"You had the same idea I did," she said, pointing to his expensive running shoes. Asher gestured down the dirt path a short distance from the street. It was soon cut off by the fog around them, curling in wisps and giving everything an ethereal air.

She purposely studied the trees and *not* the appealing image he projected. "My time zones are all off. It's midnight or thereabouts where we were but the sun is up here."

"It's more like nine p.m. back home, but yes. I was up and the room is too small, so I went for a run. I didn't think you'd be awake, or I would have woken you up. I guess we both needed some exercise and fresh air."

It would have been fun to run together. In the few weeks she'd been in Los Angeles, he had gone to the gym with his Native American friend. If Lenno didn't have such a dislike for her, she would have joined Asher there.

"Well, I'm going to head off. Is that a good path?"

He nodded and fell into step with her. "I can go again, if you want some company."

She did and she didn't, and she wasn't going to tell Asher that. "Sure."

The mist snatched away any perspiration she might have had, but as they jogged in silence, she could feel the sweat gather in the dark places on her body. She enjoyed a healthy sweat as much as anyone, when it was on the delicious Asher. They could shower together, taking turns under the nozzle and…this was not good.

Euryale forced her mind away from the enticing thought of Asher naked and wet.

* * *

The city center of Mallow was as quaint as the inn they inhabited. Even in this foggy chill morning, there were people out, bustling around from their cars to their shops, delivering items, getting their stores ready for the morning. Asher wondered how many in this village were banshees, or those who helped the banshees. The air of otherness lay as heavy over the area as the fog that was still curling around their feet. They couldn't see more than fifty feet in front of them but that was okay with him. All he needed was Euryale.

He had never expected to feel gut-punched by the Gorgon, but the more time he spent with her, the more time he enjoyed spending with her. There was something more to her, a pride and an arrogance that spoke of her being a goddess. He wondered now at the wisdom of bringing her with him to talk to Clíodhna.

They jogged out of the main city center and back to the grass paths that lined the edge of the town. Asher glanced at the woman by his side, who returned his regard with a solemn air. His breath whooshed out of him in a way that had nothing to do with this second jog of the day. In his hundred years, he'd had girlfriends and had even gotten married once, but he didn't think he'd ever experienced this. It was like a low burn in his gut that touching her would alleviate. Yet he would not. He couldn't touch her, getting involved was *not* part of the plan. They were here for a mission and that was all. She had a job to do as a condition of having her curse lifted and that was the reason she spent time with him. Otherwise, she had a world to explore without fearing that others would detect her real face. There were many gods who would want a goddess like her on their side. The fact that Athena had cursed her would be a bonus to other pantheons. Plus, once he was done and the favor fulfilled, he had a whole new life to live. But if he didn't fulfill it, his life or his mother's life would be forfeit. He had to remember that and not get distracted by Euryale's sex appeal.

"You're quiet," she said, and he slowed to a walk. She fell into an easy pace beside him. Their hands brushed on the narrow path, sending a jolt of sensation through his fingers.

"I vocalize all day for my job," he said. There was no way he could tell her the real reason. "Sometimes it's nice to just be."

She glanced up at him. "There were months, perhaps years, although time blurs when you're immortal, when I didn't speak to anyone except cave rats and the occasional wild animals. I appreciate silence."

Their hands brushed again. Asher would never know what impulse took him to act on his desire, but he slid his palm into hers. Euryale's breath caught before she let him take her hand.

"How did you stand it?" He asked the question, hoping she would think that he was offering solace. She was beautiful, tragic, so many things that made his protective instincts flare.

A shadow passed across her body, like a weight on her soul. "You endure because you have to. I had no choice. Sometimes my sister and I would be together, but when we were, it only served to remind us of what was done to us. It's an odd thing being a monster. We were still us, but we also weren't. We lived in the moment. I could go weeks without remembering I was once a goddess, not a monster. It was easier that way. Then I would remember, and the loss would slam into me again. That was in the early days. After centuries you become resigned to your fate. Sometimes I couldn't imagine what it had been like to live as a human."

"You adjusted back pretty fast."

"When humans started building more and more cities and I retained the ability to appear 'human' among them, I took advantage. I prowled the alleys in search of murderers and crooks to make my meal. It is funny what humans will do when they come across a helpless woman."

Asher shuddered at this remembrance of Euryale's bestial side. There was more than one reason that Athena had selected the Gorgons to help with this cause.

She gave him a sidelong glance. "If you're thinking I'm a murderer, you would be right. I had enough humanity in me not to kill the innocent, but I took plenty of mortals for meals—and enjoyed them, too. If that bothers you, we should go our separate ways and meet in Albania. I could leave now."

She went to tug her hand away, but Asher held on even as she used her strength to try and break free. He whirled her toward him. Despair played across her face before she shuttered it to studied blankness. He tried to dip into her mind but was repelled by her shields.

"Fuck, Elexis. That's a leap worth of your talents that you took there. I never said anything about being disgusted. "It's"—he paused, trying to find the right word—"kind of fascinating, if you want the truth. Beasts in the primal now, in touch with nature in ways humans can't."

To his relief, she relaxed her straining arm and let her hand stay within his. Her musk tantalized his nostrils with the faint tinge of the feminine, secretive, and wild. For a moment, he wished he could have glimpsed her as a beast. It was intriguing to wonder at the enigma that was Euryale.

"I'm still a monster to some," she said and turned her troubled dark gaze to meet his. "Many in the supernatural world have witnessed us as fiends over the centuries and they will not forget it. I menaced more than one god in my time."

He grinned and stepped closer. Her hair lay in damp strands across her neck and he reached for a lock, pushing it back and taking the opportunity to slide his hand around her skin. He grazed his lips over hers and heard her indrawn breath with a grateful feeling low in his gut. Her body trembled, and he hoped with everything in him that that was desire talking. She tasted of the morning air and a faint brininess. Her body was smooth and warm. He could press her to him and take everything she had to offer. His hands shook with the need to touch her. Before he could stop himself, he took her hand and pressed his palm against hers.

"I bet the gods deserved it. They're all assholes."

"Be careful who you insult there."

Chapter Seven

Clíodhna—for it could only be her—was a slender woman of indeterminate age. Standing about five feet away from them, she appeared at one with the Mallow countryside. Her thick, light-brown hair was braided into two plaits. Her dress and cloak were the green of nature and floated in the foggy air. Next to her was a woman who bore a resemblance to Asher in the cut of her cheekbones and the strength of her brow. The difference in hair color—hers was redder than Clíodhna's, gave her pale skin a ruddy glow that Asher's lacked.

Euryale cleared her throat and tried to step back, but Asher held onto her hand as he had before.

"Goddess," Euryale murmured. While she did not care for other gods, when you were in their country, it was polite to respect them. The other alternative would be to growl, and though she had growled at gods over the centuries, they needed this one's help. Besides, her growls could be put to much better use. Like bed play with Asher.

"Euryale," Clíodhna returned and inclined her head to the Gorgon. Euryale liked that she used her true name and warmed a bit to this Irish goddess. Clíodhna and the Tuatha dé Danann were…unusual. Perhaps she wouldn't be so bad.

"Asher," Clíodhna continued and gestured for him to come forward. He shot her a glance and Euryale released his hand. He moved within Clíodhna's clutches. Euryale's countenance narrowed with the desire to rip him away from the goddess and any woman who dared touch Asher. He was hers.

He was *hers*.

His mother, and Euryale struggled with the name before she came up with it—Roisin, stood impassively while the goddess reached for Asher. Clíodhna had a timeless quality that all the great ones possessed. Euryale was quite sure the same wasn't true of her. She watched Clíodhna without blinking, one goddess to another.

"You look a fine thing, son of Roisin," Clíodhna said, gripping Asher's shoulders before kissing him on first one cheek and then another. "You've been away too long." She regarded Asher with somber brown eyes that were the color of old tree bark before stepping back and turning her attention to Euryale. To Euryale's surprise, she bowed her head in a gesture of respect, one equal to another. Euryale had not expected it from the Queen of the Banshees. Clíodhna was greeting Euryale as if she were one of the Tuatha dé Danann.

"Goddess," Euryale said, inclining her head.

"You've got my banshees in a twist, Euryale," Clíodhna said.

"I am a Gorgon." Euryale inclined her head as Clíodhna had. "We were once much feared in the pantheon, even if we were not among the great gods."

"Mother." Asher was saying, embracing the other woman. If Euryale had had any doubt of who she was, the gesture took away that uncertainty. Asher was not given to frivolous emotional gestures.

"It's good to see you, son. I've missed you so. It's been a long time."

His face fell like she had given him the rough edge of her tongue, although her words were mild.

"It has been," he agreed and kissed first one cheek and then the other. "I didn't think about it. We always have time."

"Away with you," she replied, her eyes hooded. "Not anymore."

Euryale's breath caught, remembering what Asher had said. His life or his mother's life, or both, were forfeit if he did not do this task.

Clíodhna gestured to Asher, who linked his arm with his mother's.

"Come, we have to have a chinwag. You need to be told more about this wee enemy of the gods, the one you have been sent to find."

Asher cleared his throat. His enchantment at the sight of the great Tuatha dé Danann goddess made Euryale's jealousy flare to life. She had not been jealous in a human way in centuries and the emotion was unsettling.

"We do want your counsel, Clíodhna, Queen. But we were also told that you asked to speak to us. How can we be of assistance?"

* * *

Euryale was behaving oddly. There was no other way to describe it. She followed behind as they made their way to Clíodhna's cottage. They were still in their running clothes as the goddess had said there was no need to change. It didn't bother Asher and didn't appear to concern Euryale. Something else was awry, he could detect it in her stiff posture.

Women. Who could figure them? He shot a glance at his mother, but if she had anything to say, she offered nothing. She nodded at him and pressed closer.

Clíodhna ushered them inside where two women greeted them and offered refreshments. He could tell they were both banshees by their mental signature and they were helpers, or servants to the goddess. Clíodhna had always been more of a mysterious figurehead in the distance. Now she was real, and she was in front of him. For once in his life he was at a loss for words. He had met many supernatural beings in America, but few old gods.

"I would have a word with you about your quest. First, I'll wet the tea," Clíodhna said when they were settled with tea and biscuits. The tea was poured from a delicate pot that had the appearance of a family heirloom. More than likely, that family was Clíodhna. It had been decades since he had encountered her, but she hadn't changed. She'd always had the appearance of a woman on her way to middle age who was still nonetheless agile and strong. Like his mother. He'd never been told how old Roisin was, only that it was somewhere between his relative youth and the timeless age of the two great goddesses occupying the cottage.

It was Euryale who spoke. "We are, of course, desiring of your wise counsel," she demurred, sipping her tea. "We did not come on this errand of our own accord, however. We were summoned to perform this task. We were, how shall we say, drafted?"

To his surprise, Clíodhna laughed. In that laugh was the edge of a banshee in the rising wail. Her howl would be the stuff of legends, far stronger than the others. There was great power in her voice. It might have the ability to bring down gods.

"Aye, you were, like. Roisin came to me when Ares informed her that the long-ago pact had been put into motion. The problem of these god murders affects all of us. We lost Cian, which was a holy show. He was stronger, like, than they thought, and he is coming back to life now, though he is not the full shilling yet. It was not as effective as they may have intended."

Euryale tilted her head in silent query. It was Roisin who hastened to explain after a nod at Clíodhna. The goddess inclined her head, granting permission.

"Cian is the son of Dian Cecht, the Tuatha dé Danann god of healing. He is a minor god in this pantheon, and some would say not a god at all. He was struck down and is only now coming back to life. I would have told you sooner, but I just learned of it." Roisin's next glance at her goddess almost held censure.

"I didn't realize they had affected the Tuatha dé Danann until you called," Asher said with a rueful twist to his lips. "I was not aware of these assassins until the Greek gods pressed us into service. Someone should have told me sooner."

Clíodhna nodded, sipping her tea. One of the women bustled in at Clíodhna's actions to tend to the goddess's needs but she waved the woman away. The woman glared back at Asher, and disapproval flashed across her face before she turned away with an audible sniff.

"It's a right mess, but you knowing would have changed nothing. It was decided not to reveal what had happened to outsiders, but now, with your quest, it's time. As for Cian, it is not as hard to kill those with diluted blood, but it is still a feat."

Those with diluted blood. Like all demigods. The slayers had sharpened their skills on the weaker before turning their attention to the ones they were after. The Greek gods had to fear they were targets, or they wouldn't have taken the drastic step of bringing Asher and Euryale to the task.

"Cian is a favorite of mine and I would have his would-be killers punished. They have been operating in the shadows for years. We could find no trace of them other than their handiwork. I had to assure myself that you were the right one for the job. Just because you were pressed into service doesn't mean you are up to the task."

"My Queen!" Roisin's protest was loud and shrill.

Clíodhna sipped her tea.

"And if he wasn't?"

Euryale's tone was challenging, and the goddess raised an eyebrow. Asher had to remind himself that Euryale, too, was a goddess.

"We cannot afford for him to make a hash of it. If he does, then the banshees must take up the battle. This cannot go unanswered. Asher, you will find help in unexpected locations. We are many places where people do not think we can be. Too often, older women are disregarded. It is to our benefit to remain, as you Americans say, under the radar. You may need allies and we will provide them. Just don't eff it up."

That seemed to satisfy his mother, although she was still stiff with indignation at his side. He could feel a wail growing in his throat, a desire to howl at their queen, but he resisted. Asher had no doubt that Clíodhna could top whatever he could do, and more.

"You are a goddess," Euryale continued, "Does Asher have a way of getting in touch with you if he needs you? I don't mind telling you that I'm happy to know we're not completely alone."

She looked from the goddess to the man and Asher paused, and then glanced at his mother.

"I can reach out if I need to, no matter the distance. I think…I think you will be watching, my Queen, is that right?"

Clíodhna gave him an approving nod. "It is, young Asher. I was concerned you were not up to this task, but I may have been mistaken. There is more to you than meets the eye. Your god blood is a potent mixture with banshee stock. And you, Gorgon, you are quite unexpected."

Euryale said nothing for a moment, studying Clíodhna. The other goddess neither blinked nor stirred, and Asher wondered if they were communicating without words.

"So, if we need help, then all we have to do is call for one of you?"

Clíodhna appraised Euryale for more long, silent moments and Asher speculated what they were saying to each other. He could get nothing from behind their shields.

"If you are in need of assistance, we will be there. You have been elected to fight this battle and we would not take that glory. But you are not going in alone. If the need arises, we will find you." She extended a hand toward Roisin. "There is nothing more potent than a mother protecting her child. In this sense, the banshees are all your mothers."

"What would be better is identifying who or what we're trying to find. That, and some teeth and claws." Euryale did *not* appear to be kidding.

Clíodhna appeared to consider Euryale's statement with the same gravity that the other goddess had. "Your centuries as a beast have not yet faded. That may prove to be an asset. I wish there was more I could tell you, but Cian's mind is clouded from the attack and he remembers little of it. Just that he heard a high, piercing wail, and then he…exploded. It was gruesome, from what the Morrigan said. Those women love the blood, which cheesed the banshees off." Clíodhna also didn't appear disturbed by the idea. "He is not quite himself yet, or I would have had you meet with him."

"How long do you think these people have been murdering gods?" Asher set his cup down. He didn't like that they hadn't received this information until it started affecting the major pantheons.

Clíodhna's gaze went to the horizon, her face shadowed. "A decade or longer. We are gods, Asher. Time has little meaning for us. There is a method and a reason for what these killers are doing. Discover that and you will find them."

He studied the goddess. "Fair enough. But once we do, how do we stop them?"

She returned his gaze, but he couldn't read her face. "That is the mystery, son of Ares."

* * *

"She could have been more helpful," Euryale said as they headed back to the airport. She was edgy. It would be good to go back to a cave and forget this stupidity. The idea that there was a god killer out there affected her just as much. They could decide to turn on Stheno next, or her vulnerable mortal sister. Whoever these people were, they had to be stopped.

Asher shot her a quizzical glance. "You're not being fair. She told us what she could."

"She told us what it suited her to reveal. All gods are arrogant."

Asher glanced at the driver—his mother—and then back at Euryale. He meant it as a warning, but she didn't care.

"I resent being told I have this job to do and then not being given the tools to fix it. If I were the way I used to be, it would be easy. All we keep hearing is that this thing kills gods but not how we can defeat it."

He put a hand on her arm and gripped it.

I'm sorry we were interrupted, he mind-spoke in soothing tones. *I wanted to kiss you. I still do.*

She glanced up at him and then to Roisin. Euryale shook her head minutely, but wasn't sure if she meant the gesture as reassurance or a warning to his mother.

Who said I desired you?

Didn't you?

"Sometimes I think they are getting what they deserve," she said, ignoring his further attempts at communicating. "They are so full of themselves, so sure they can do no wrong that I think 'hah, good for whoever is doing this.'"

Asher said nothing for a moment. His hand stayed on her arm. It would be so good to put her fingers around his and urge his hand into more interesting places. This wasn't like her. She was a goddess and hadn't had any sort of normal human experience in over a thousand years. Two thousand years. She wondered what it would be like to kiss Asher in the back of this tiny car and fondle him.

"Aye, that's right," Roisin said, startling Euryale.

"Sorry?" Asher said.

She braced for attack. Roisin was agitated, which Euryale had put down to the situation. Now, after observing his mother's stony face, she wasn't so sure.

"The gods are manky bastards. Arrogant, the lot of them."

Euryale studied the woman. His mother had a brittle quality but was too well shielded for Euryale to tell what she was thinking.

"Most are, but aren't you proud of the Tuatha dé Danann and Clíodhna?" Asher continued. "She is our queen."

The woman made an inelegant snort. "Aye, like, but you are my son. I'm not coddling you now, we're in it, no going back. I've made a right mess of things and all we can do now is set it right. I'd take it back if I could."

Asher's attention wavered between his mother and at the woman sitting so close. Finally, he focused on the woman who had given birth to him. "It would have happened sooner or later. This day was always going to come."

"Aye, but I would have tried to stall the ball if I could have. Too late for regrets. You have to go beyond and fix it. I would go in your place, but Ares would not hear of it. It's you, like, and that's that. The manky eejit said it to me this way: 'We cannot allow these enemies of the gods to continue. If they are allowed to go unchecked, then all the pantheons are threatened.'" She sighed and passed a hand over her eyes. "It's right hard being a supernatural being these days."

Euryale let out a long, scoffing sound and rolled her eyes. "Why do we need the gods?"

The woman laughed with a bitter, howling edge. "They are the grandest spirits among us. There are many mysteries in this world, but the immortal gods hold it all together."

"They are just as capricious as humans."

"Aye, and who taught the humans?"

Euryale mulled this over for a few silent minutes and then inclined her head.

"You have a point." She wished she had kissed Asher in the fog. It would have been glorious.

"We need the gods. They need us too, though they'd never admit it. We are all part of a whole and cannot afford a wobble. It's jam on your egg to think it could be different. This is yours and yours alone."

Euryale snorted at that. "Why don't all the gods come together to stop this if it is that big of a threat? It could not stand against so many."

"Try getting two gods to agree on anything, even our own. Fat chance we could get several powerful pantheons to reach an agreement. I asked our queen this question and that was her answer."

She considered this and then inclined her head again. "She's right. But there should be more of us. Why only two?"

Roisin shrugged. "It's not clear to any of us. Perhaps it's because you're unexpected. These god killers are expecting more than a banshee and a Gorgon. If I were killing gods, I would be waiting for Olympus, ah, but they'd only make a hash of it. Asher, when the milling starts, I will be there if you need me."

Asher reached out from the back seat and put his hand on his mother's shoulder. "Thank you, Mother, but I would not put you in danger," he said. "You're the first one to offer assistance. Everyone else is just telling us what to do."

The woman's gaze once again met theirs, her face a stony mask. "Aye, and you will get more of that. They underestimate anyone who is not like them. I love you, son, and you have my aid if you need it. You have my word."

Chapter Eight

Tirana, Albania, lay on the Adriatic Sea between Montenegro, Macedonia, Kosovo, and Greece. Euryale had spent time here as a monster and was acquainted with the coastline and some of the hidden places. The Albanian Alps were an ideal hiding place for one such as her. Among the rocks and crags there had been numerous sites to make her home. But she had moved on, as she always did.

"What can you tell me about this pantheon?" Asher asked as they emerged into the bright sunshine of the capital city. Tirana was like many other ancient cities—part modern and part buildings steeped in antiquity. As the biggest city by far in Albania, as well as being the capital, Tirana had the lion's share of the tourists. It was located in the center of the country surrounded by mountains and hills, with Dajt on the east and overlooking the Adriatic Sea in the distance. Due to its location within the Tirana plain and the close proximity to the Adriatic Sea, the city was influenced by a Mediterranean seasonal climate. The monster in her basked in the sunshine it offered.

"It's been centuries since I've been here," Euryale said and glanced at Asher. "I've always liked Albania. Their pantheon was kind to me, for a while. I stayed here and in some of the other countries, the ones now called Bulgaria and something else, I can't recall, for quite a while. My sister did as well."

"Don't you want to visit with her?"

Euryale studied the bustling city traffic and took note of the clock tower that was one of Tirana's landmarks, dating from Ottoman Empire times. She gestured to nothing in particular. "Stheno, aka Saskia, and I have an understanding. She is still getting used to being in her human form. Egypt suits her, for the moment.

If I need her, she will be there, and vice versa. I wouldn't put her in the middle of this danger unless I had no other option. She is taking care that Medusa does not come to harm. That is something I cannot do, given the situation. She is going where she is most needed. If things go wrong, she will come."

His brows furrowed together. "But it was your bargain with Athena that allowed both of you to become your original selves. Isn't she grateful?"

Euryale laughed, a harsh, grating sound. "Stheno is a fierce warrior and the claws and snakes were her weaponry. She enjoys the perks of being a goddess, but part of her wouldn't mind staying a monster. If I have little love for Athena, she has less. Sometimes it's easier to recognize what to do when you are inhuman."

His raised eyebrows showed he didn't understand, so she turned her attention to the landscape. Tirana's buildings were pastel colored, in pink and yellow shades with greens and blues poking among the other colors. Multicolored awnings covered storefronts. The streets were clogged with cars, motorcyclists, and foot traffic.

His dark hair fell over his forehead in an endearing gesture. She needed to push that lock of hair back and stroke him. Euryale jerked her hand away as soon as she was aware she'd raised it to do just that. She didn't have the right to touch him, and even if she did, it was a stupid thing to do to get all gushy over a man. That was what had gotten Medusa—and them—into trouble. She should stay focused on the task at hand. She had no business thinking about a man and a future.

He took her elbow to guide her through foot traffic.

"The tour books suggest Skandberg Square as a destination, but I believe it is still being remodeled," she said, and Asher gave her a blank stare.

"What is that?" he asked.

She pointed in the opposite direction of where they were heading. "It's a square built around one of Albania's heroes. I investigated it while we were getting ready because it's a nice open space. It felt like a probable spot for the pantheon to meet us. It's being turned into some sort of pedestrian park and is off limits."

He still appeared blank.

"The Albanians may not be willing to help us," she admitted with a rueful edge to her voice.

"We won't get that answer until we ask them," he replied. "I also did some reading. There's a place called the Friendship Monument not too far from Et'Hem Bej Mosque. Why don't we go there?"

She found herself taking his arm without even knowing she was doing it until they were skin to skin.

"Mosque and Friendship Monument, it is. Asher, you are full of surprises."

* * *

The Friendship Monument was a shaded structure that commemorated the eternal friendship between Albania and Kuwait. Asher didn't know much about the region, and even less about its history. Until that moment, he hadn't realized that there was an "eternal friendship" between Albania and Kuwait. If a person dug into his past, they would find a forged high school diploma, always kept current. In his line of work, he didn't need a college degree, but people didn't take anyone without basic education seriously. World history hadn't been interesting to him, until now.

"This isn't much to speak of," he observed when they arrived at the indicated place. There was a commemorative plaque, and at the top, appeared to be balloons. Tirana was a mix of Ottoman, Soviet, and Italian influences. He knew as little about the city as he did about its pantheon.

They took refuge under the round structure as a light rain fell. He'd learned that Tirana was a rainy city, but also warm, and today was no exception. As the mist continued, he imagined more people would gather in the monument, but they stayed away from the edifice. There were two, in addition to them, taking refuge there. No others approached as the precipitation began to fall harder.

"What can you tell me about the pantheon? What should we expect from their gods?"

Euryale put her hands on the bench. She caressed its surface and he desired her hands to be stroking him instead. He needed to feel and touch her warm, strong body. He shouldn't be letting this unexpected attraction get in the way. He needed to focus, to do this favor for Ares, and then he and his family would be done with the Greeks. He had no business being attracted to a former monster, no matter how pretty the package. But all he could think about was Euryale. Touching her. Feeling her. Being inside her.

He'd lost the thread of her conversation. "Sorry, what was that?"

She gave him a grin and there was a lazy sensuality in there that made his breath catch. Soon his desire was going to be obvious.

"Their gods are part of a pagan tradition. There is Baba Tomor, the father of all gods and humans in the Albanian mythology. I've never met him, but I hear he's cranky. He often manifests as an old man. I think he likes it that way. There's Prende, the goddess of love and beauty. There's Enji, the god of fire. Perendi, the thunder god. Shurdhi and Verbti, weather gods. There are others, but I don't recall them all. They are not worshiped too much these days, although they are not forgotten."

"We are not so forgotten," a new voice said, and Asher spun around. The couple who'd stayed behind gave them expectant glances. Euryale swore, an unfamiliar word that nonetheless made its meaning clear.

"I should have been aware of this before now." She rose and Asher went with her. Together they faced the duo, a man and a woman. The woman was wearing a hijab, but underneath the headdress was a face of such startling beauty that she could only be a goddess. The man was slight but with a solid frame that would be stronger than it appeared if put to the test.

"Who are they?" Asher addressed Euryale; his gaze was on the new pair.

"Prende and Enji, hello," she said with a disgusted sound.

"Gorgon, you should be more careful in your tone with gods," Enji said. He was a tall man with a short beard that held specks of silver. "Athena is not the only one with the power to transform."

Asher stared at the man whose gaze was fixed on Euryale. There was something contemptuous about his glare that was disproportionate to their first meeting. Euryale met his gaze with a defiant shake of her hair, then lowered it and scratched at the stone floor with her foot.

Then she looked up and her expression was wry. She glanced at Asher who drew his eyebrows together and tried to send her a question, but her mind was shuttered.

"I am not that monster of a few centuries ago," she said. "I am back in my original form."

He blew out a breath. "You were a monster before. You ate our livestock where it was not yours to eat."

She scuffed the ground with her shoe. "I was hungry. You did not need so many."

Enji was not as tall as Asher but carried an aura of authority. He spat his next words. "They were our goats."

"I could have done worse."

"You risk the anger of the pantheon, Gorgon."

"Fuck," Asher swore. "Elexis…" Why hadn't she told him she wasn't welcome in Albania. They could have found another way.

"Her name is Euryale, banshee, and you would do well not to forget that."

They were all speaking in English, although he doubted it was their preferred language. He had the god's knack of being able to understand all languages but was most comfortable in his adopted tongue. It was a courtesy he wouldn't have expected from this pair, given their anger toward Euryale.

"She asked to be called Elexis and I respect that."

"There is much about this Gorgon that doesn't deserve veneration."

Euryale blew out a breath and then bobbed her head. "You are right, Enji. I owe you my apologies. I had no business interfering with your lives all those centuries ago. We were all stronger then and I was…angry."

There was more to the story, Asher understood, and vowed to find out once this was over. His slow simmer of anger at her withholding information was going to have to wait as well. They had a job to do. For now, he waited to see what Enji and Prende would do. If they refused to help, this was going to be a short trip.

"I accept your apology for the moment, Gorgon. Once our business is done, do not come within our borders unless invited. It will not go well for you a second time."

Her face hardened, and Euryale opened her mouth to either argue or lunge at Enji. After a moment Euryale inclined her head, her stony features unmoving. By the twist of her lips, he could tell she was trying to control her temper.

It came flooding back to Asher now, the folly of being attracted to Euryale. She was a monster, had been one for longer than he could imagine. He was stupid to want to slide inside her.

"We have a job to do, Enji. Thank you for your courtesy. I'm Asher, and we're on a common mission. It's to all the gods' benefit that we find this person or persons before they strike again. I'm not familiar with the history of your anger at Elex…Euryale, but we have to put all that aside and work toward our common cause."

Prende leaned over and whispered something to Enji. The man's face softened for a moment and he nodded.

He didn't glance in Euryale's direction when he spoke again. "Indeed, son of Ares. Need overrides all other consideration. Come. Walk with us. We have much to discuss."

Asher glanced up at the sky where the rain was falling harder.

"Shurdhi is keeping the rain up for us," Enji said. "It was his brother who was slain. Verbti is starting to show signs of returning but he is still lost."

Asher struggled to remember what Euryale said about who the gods were. *Weather gods.*

He breathed out a sigh of relief that she was once again available to him in his mind. Asher dared to regard Euryale, but she was studying Enji. The man met her gaze, and for a moment, there was something else there. A flare of jealousy shot through Asher. What had Enji and Euryale been to each other?

"We will walk with you," Asher said and offered his hand to Euryale, who took it. Prende slipped her hand around Enji's elbow and they walked into the rain.

* * *

It had been a long time ago and Euryale hoped Enji had forgotten. Gods had long memories and rarely forgot a slight, or an injury.

"We are members of the local government here." Prende was saying, her face unreadable. Her mind was closed to Euryale but that was fine with her. She didn't trust goddesses and this one was vain and unpredictable. Just like a beautiful goddess was expected to be. She should have anticipated that Enji and Prende would be the ones to "greet" them. Tomor would let the gods who had tangled with Euryale take the lead again.

Asher nodded, a perfunctory gesture. He did not understand or, to her relief, care about her history with the Albanian gods. She was sure he would want to be told more later.

The rain was heavier now, though it did not touch the gods. Shurdhi was one of their major pantheons and had precision ability with his weather talent. She had not encountered him in her last sojourn to Albania, but that had been a long time ago.

Euryale, on the other hand, was getting soaked as was Asher. The rain was saturating her clothes and had already sodden her hair, which now lay in clumps across her neck. Another bit of petty revenge on the part of the Albanian gods.

She had only scratched Enji. It was a mere slash on his chest, and it healed. It wasn't worth fussing over.

Asher's outfit was clinging to his body in interesting and delightful ways. His chest and leg muscles stood out against the cloth, showing again how well-built he was. A primitive desire stirred within her, more akin to the monster she used to be than the restored goddess she was now.

"Being part of government is a smart way to keep suspicion off you. You can't stay in it forever. How do you explain your lack of aging after a few decades?"

"Albania has become more democratic," Enji said with a shrug. "We are still able to disguise our reality, although it is unclear how much longer we can keep it up. We do not aspire to the highest government, that would be too public. We take local seats where we can influence the politics around us. The humans are not aware they are being affected."

"I imagine that must rankle gods like Tomor," she said and earned a sharp stare from Prende.

"Do not think we have forgotten what you did here, Gorgon," she said, her beautiful face creasing into unhappy lines. "Do not think you are welcome here. It was expedience and need that allowed you to come here at all. We work for the common good of all of us; otherwise we would not have allowed you to set foot in our territory."

She opened her mouth to speak but Asher beat her to it.

"Not welcome?" He asked the question with the sort of incredulity that came with someone who was offended. "We are here to *help*, and you say she should not be here? You're idiots." Even though they were the full-blood gods and he the half blood, for a moment, he swelled taller than all of them, his outrage lending him strength.

Euryale was thrilled at his defense of her and almost let him continue, but they couldn't afford to anger any more deities. She'd done enough damage.

"I apologize for my behavior in my other form," she said, and Asher swiveled his head to stare at her, indignation written all over him.

"You should," Prende sniffed. "We may be a trifling pantheon, but we are not to be trifled with. You…hurt us."

Her heart sank. They needed the information the Albanians had about the killers. She nodded her head and then bowed.

"I apologize, with all my heart and the power of a goddess," she said. "Does that satisfy you?"

Prende and Enji were quiet, but she could detect them mind-speaking for several moments. She shuffled next to Asher, but despite his probe, did not let him into her mind. She would do what she had to do, to protect their return to humanity, and her sister's safety.

"It will suffice," Enji said. "We will require more of you, a penance, but now is not the time."

Euryale breathed out a sigh of relief.

"Tell us what you can about the people who killed Verbti."

Chapter Nine

Euryale had not been to Athens in fifteen hundred years and had never expected to return. Yet here she was, in a cramped hotel room with Asher that made up for its tiny square footage by a stunning view of the Acropolis. She remembered a time before this ancient wonder was built, and also when it was in its glory, standing strong and proud with painted stone and beautiful statues. Now it was grey and faded, the statues gone, the carefully crafted marble, chipped and displaced. Euryale was heartened that evidence of restoration attempts were all around them in the scaffolding and cranes that were on the hill next to the monument.

"I've never been to Greece before," Asher said as they made their way down the crowded streets. They skirted a dense thicket of people and traffic as they walked to a local taverna to get a meal. Everywhere they looked the Acropolis was visible, reminding Euryale of a time when gods visited their temples. One of those visits had led to the downfall of her sister, and the Gorgons.

"There was a time when it was all that mattered in the ancient world," Euryale said, dodging a Greek Orthodox priest who murmured a blessing as they passed. "The Romans were upstarts."

He grinned and took her hand. She let him, enjoying his warm flesh against hers. There was a solidity and a feeling of home to him that was unlike anything she had ever felt. Not even with Stheno and Medusa did she feel this overwhelming sense of companionship.

"I think the Romans may have something to say about that," he murmured and pressed closer to her. They headed into the center of the city a few blocks away, to eat at a recommended place.

She made a dismissive motion with her free hand. "We were there first."

They entered the recommended location, and despite the press of humanity, they were ushered to an open table. She glanced over the prices, relieved that they were modest. Although she had some money, she couldn't afford to be frivolous.

Asher glanced over the menu. "What do you recommend? I'd try the ouzo, but I swore off alcohol after what happened in L.A. No thanks on the retsina, which is disgusting."

The waiter approached just as he said the final words and his face shifted.

"Retsina is an acquired taste and perhaps not suitable for Americans. I assure you some Greeks are very fond of it."

He sounded offended and didn't hide it. Euryale detected another low-level paranormal in his aspect, with the suggestion of inward curving horns and a bull's body. Perhaps a Bonnacon then, but she couldn't be sure. Here in the heart of Greece, the land was littered with the by-products of gods and other creatures.

"No alcohol for us," Euryale said and scanned the menu. "I'll take the octopus, and can I get some hummus and falafel to start?"

The waiter studied her for a moment. It was apparent that he had identified Euryale, at least, by the wary way he held himself and didn't meet her eyes.

"*Nai*," he said. "For the gentleman?"

Having ordered, they stared at each other. Euryale was at a loss for what to say.

"What do you think about what Enji told us?" he asked.

She toyed with her silverware, shrugging and saying many things in that simple movement. Disappointment was most prominent. "It wasn't much."

He shook his head. "It was plenty. There are at least three of them, if not more. They have some sort of weapon that tears even gods apart, perhaps sonically. It all leads back to sound, and likely explains why we were chosen. The Albanians revealed quite a bit, considering how much they dislike you."

She started and tried to cover the quick movement by picking up her glass. A grin played across his face, but Asher said nothing.

"You picked up on that, huh?"

He grinned. "It wasn't hard. Enji was oozing anger."

"I did try to kill him, but he asked for it," she admitted. "I was a monster and a goddess and it…interested him. So, we had sex and then I went for him. I just needed to have some fun."

"That was fun to you?"

"In that form it was. I was different. More primal."

"I like primal."

She blushed, using her water glass to hide the sudden flush. There was no getting around the fact that she sought to get naked with Asher more than she'd desired to be with anyone in centuries.

"I keep going back to something Prende said. She said there was a woman in charge of the mob that killed their weather god. That she was the leader."

"It fits with what we experienced in Los Angeles. That was female. It is logical that their findings are in keeping with ours. We are trying to find a group controlled by a woman. It shouldn't surprise you, Asher. Women are often more bloodthirsty than men. You let things go. We don't."

He let out a breath and inhaled again. "I've been around women all my life. That's a pretty harsh assessment."

She rounded on him, fury etched across every feature on her face. Her voice was controlled when she spoke but shook with anger. "You weren't turned into a monster for a millennium because your sister was raped in a temple by a god, and *his* sister was offended. Not that your sister was raped, but that her temple maiden was no longer pure. I have *every* right to be unforgiving."

He opened his mouth as though he would say something but then picked up his water glass and took a sip.

"Fair enough, I guess. I didn't realize how deep it still went. I'm sorry, Euryale. I didn't mean to stir old wounds. We're searching for a goddess, someone with a grudge, and with helpers who can keep a secret. There are lots of people who fit that description."

She considered him for a moment, finding truth in his words. He had meant no offense. "True. The Albanians didn't recognize whoever this was who struck at their weather god. From what I've understood, nobody has so far. Even concealed, the major pantheon is recognizable by their mental signature. That means that they are a minor god."

"Or from a minor pantheon." His brows drew together. "We don't have enough puzzle pieces to say it's a Greek goddess, yet it all fits together. Would it make more sense to be from a forgotten pantheon? They could be avenging the fact that they're disremembered in modern days."

It took her a moment to sort through her impressions. "It could be, but my instincts say no. Otherwise you couldn't have dragged me here. The Greeks are the ones leading this mission. There's a reason. This goddess has to be their own— my own. The minor pantheons don't have anyone with this type of power. They fade, and as they fade, so does their influence. If it were a mob near extinction, like the Sumerians, then I doubt Athena and Ares would have gone through all this trouble. They don't care about an Albanian weather god, or the one from the Germanic pantheon—I can't remember the name now—that appears he's dead for good. There's a reason why Athena took the drastic step of getting me and Stheno back to our full strength and godhood. They need our power. They must be afraid of whoever is doing this. That wouldn't come from the Caananite gods or the Guanche. It comes from within."

After studying her in silence for a heartbeat, Asher nodded. "When you put it that way, it makes sense. Have you detected something with your spidey senses?"

She frowned and he bounced in his seat, beaming with an inner pride. "It's a comic book thing. Never mind. All this is very well and good, but what you're saying is, it's familiar to you, and therefore it's the Greeks."

"Yes."

He tapped his fingers on the table. "Then I agree. What do we do next? We've come without a plan, but we need one."

She inclined her head. "You are right. We've been tugged around by gods without any real idea of how to go about our goal. Now we're here. I'm not sure what our next plan of action is."

She wanted to walk with him in the city streets and push him into an alley and kiss him. She sought to strip off her clothes and dance naked in front of him in their tiny hotel room and pounce on him on the single bed. Everything else faded away to points of insignificance. She could not remember a time when longing struck her this way.

"Maybe we shouldn't have come here so soon. We could have gone to Albania from Germany—since one of their pantheon was killed as well."

"If this is where we need to be, we shouldn't waste any more time." Asher slid his hand across the table to grasp hers. She let him, wishing that it didn't feel so good to touch him. Emotions had been Medusa's downfall, what had gotten her in trouble, that and, a goddess who wouldn't accept that her brother had any part in the defilement.

They waited while the waiter brought hummus and baba ghanoush, along with some hot pita bread. Euryale's stomach rumbled, a reminder that it had been a while since she had eaten. Goddess she may be, but she had to fill her belly just like humans did. As her other self did. Except her monster didn't care for niceties, whereas as a woman, Euryale found herself watching her manners.

She was opening her mouth to say something, when everything around them shattered.

* * *

It happened in slow motion. First Asher was admiring the sight of Euryale's wavy brown hair glowing under the dim lights of the tavern, and then the front window was imploding. There appeared to be a sonic boom heading toward the restaurant, but he didn't have time to wonder how he could detect that before the glass began splintering. Asher grabbed Euryale and dragged her over the table and then flipped it over, so they were both crouched behind it. He threw himself around Euryale's body, shielding her from the shards that were beginning to rain down on the patrons and staff alike. People began screaming, a shrill sound of panic and fear as the clients scattered. One of the waiters tossed his tray toward the window, trying to stop the onslaught of glass that was penetrating people's bodies. Euryale began to rise to step in and help but he held her down. She could be mad at him later, but for now he would defend her. There was a series of thuds as the missiles struck their table. Others were hit by the shards, blood pouring from their wounds. Their waiter was crouched below another table. The man met his eyes, and there was such fierce anger in them, that Asher recoiled. Images of a bull with horns flickered over the man's countenance before he returned to human. Patrons ran screaming in all directions, toward the back and the front, arms flailing and stumbling over other people and objects strewn about the floor. Some went sprawling over prone bodies. Asher couldn't tell if anyone was wounded; it was too soon for that. He could feel Euryale's quick breathing against his chest as she once again tried to rise.

Then a scream began in his mind and reached fever pitch. His ears buzzed and then rang as the sonic assault went on and on. He strengthened his shield and the force ebbed from his mind, although he could still hear it pummeling his senses at a higher frequency than humans could hear. The many abandoned dogs in Athens began to howl, their yips frightened and stark. He glanced at Euryale, and he assumed she'd also put up her shields to protect her from the blast. Shielded, they were protected from the sound, but they couldn't mind-speak, which was a distinct disadvantage.

Euryale pushed at Asher and rose. She grabbed his hand and gestured toward the door. "That's a call to battle. Let's go."

He grabbed her arm to shove her back down behind the table, but there was no stopping this fierce woman. Instead he took her hand and ran with her into the night. A crowd had started to gather. They gaped at the couple but lost interest as the two sped away from the scene. Behind them, the front window was gone, nothing but shards of glass remained, and several people were scattered on the floor. The entire taverna was upended with broken tables and plants and debris all around them.

They dove through the late-night crush, still thick at this hour, and away from the taverna. They sprinted without stopping until they were several blocks away from the site, before Euryale tugged on his hand to stop. The Parthenon still glowed high above them, a beacon, regardless of where you stood in Athens.

"For fuck's sake, what was that?" he asked when they slowed and then stopped. "Any ideas?"

She shook her head in the negative and then paused and nodded. "Yes. No. Maybe. I don't think it was meant to slay. They have a great deal of power. If killing us was what they were after, they wouldn't have sent an attack like that, they would have assaulted us. It was a warning. Or a trap."

She gave him a quick once-over, her breathing ragged. Adrenaline was pumping through his body and he suspected the same was true of her.

"They want to tell us that just as we are here, so are they. They're arrogant after their successes and they think they can win. They are toying with us like cats with mice."

She bared her teeth, and there was so much menace in that gesture, that he took an involuntary step backward.

Then she kissed him. She stepped into his personal space, slid her arms around him, and pressed her lips to his. There was no artifice in the kiss, just need and raw passion. Asher's body surged to life. With a groan, he kissed her back, sliding his lips along hers as he tugged her against him. She was warm and lithe and female. She was goddess and woman and partner wrapped into one. She was heaven mixed with a slice of devil, and he had never wanted anyone so much in his entire life. It was surprising to be kissing her after they'd just fled for their lives, but he wasn't about to say no. He'd hoped to do this since the day he'd flown her back to Los Angeles. Timing didn't matter. His friend's dislike didn't concern him. All that mattered was the way she was nibbling at his lips, like he was the meal they didn't get to eat, and breathing warm air into his mouth before she tasted him again. She was the aggressor and it was glorious. His body responded, his cock rising, nudging against her leg as it hardened and she moaned, whether in reply to that feeling or something else, he wasn't sure. All that mattered was that she was in his arms and returning his ardor with equal passion.

"Shouldn't we be trying to protect ourselves?" he asked when they broke apart. His mind was reeling, and he struggled to hold onto any semblance of reality. "They could be coming for us even now."

"True," she said. "If they are, bring it on. There was something of the skirmish in this attack, as though a greater battle is coming. We might have been foolish to come to Greece so soon, since that is where they expected us to be. Remember back in Los Angeles when they were searching for us? I am familiar with this mind, but it's been centuries. It's going to take me a little bit of time to recall who and where I dealt with it before."

"How can you be so sure?"

They were still well shielded so he couldn't sense anything from her other than surface emotions, but he understood that she was serious when she peered at him.

"I'm a goddess. I've interacted with these gods and all the pantheons for millennia. Do not underestimate them, or me. After Perseus slew my sister, there was more than one idiot who believed that going after the other Gorgons was a way of making their names infamous. Don't forget, in our monster form we also had claws and snakes for hair. We constantly had to fight for our lives at first, once he went after Medusa. Now Stheno and Euryale are just footnotes to Medusa's story, but it wasn't always that way."

She was thousands of years old and a goddess. His paltry hundred years made him an infant compared to her.

"Elexis, I…" He stopped, unsure of what he was trying to say.

She took his hands in hers, her expression earnest. "Two things. First, I asked to be called Elexis, but I don't need that name anymore. There is no point in hiding. Call me Euryale. That is my name and I am proud of it. Secondly," she said and grazed a kiss over his lips. "I want to make love to you. Let's go back to the hotel."

Chapter Ten

She waited for Asher's response.

"I want to so bad," he said and grabbed her hand. "But what if they come back while we're doing the deed?"

"I can multitask," she said and touched another kiss to his lips.

Before she could say anything else, he swung her into his arms and held her close. "Let's go," he said, and she grinned.

When they got back to the hotel, he banged the door closed and shoved one of the single beds across the doorway.

"In case anyone tries to break in," he said with a mischievous gleam in his eyes.

She couldn't keep from smiling. She thought she had lost the ability to feel giddy, but with Asher it was different.

"Come here," he then growled and drew her onto the narrow single bed. The room was even tinier with his large presence filling it. Outside their window the Parthenon glittered, reminding her of where they were, and who she was. All that was for tomorrow.

Tonight was for them.

She pushed him down on the bed and straddled his waist. She kept a part of her mind alert for any possible danger in the same way that her former bestial self had once done: a piece of her aware of the outside world, while she was pleasuring herself with a willing man or beast.

"You're gorgeous," he said and there was no pretense in his voice. He was all passion and need, his body arching toward her as she raked her nails over his still-clothed chest.

"You're mine," she murmured and leaned down to kiss him. His tongue lashed out to spear inside her mouth, tasting her. She gave as good as she got, savoring him as well, their tongues tangling for long moments in a dance of desire. She lay over him and pressed against him, her contours flowing into his.

"You're the one who's mine," he said, running his hands over her back and pressing against her ass. He urged her into him so she could feel the fullness of his erection. Her former self beat inside her, telling her to strip and plunge down on him, filling herself with his hardness. Her newfound humanity savored the first moment in centuries that she'd made love as a woman and not a beast. For a moment she wasn't sure which side would win out.

She sighed and relaxed into him. Asher accepted the embrace, his hands stilling on her back. That he felt her struggle made her want him all the more in human, woman ways of love and need, of caring and concern, of passion and desire mixed together. The complexities of her emotions scared her a little, but her craving won out over such minor considerations.

"I want you," she breathed, rising again and pressing a kiss to his lips.

He ran his hands down her back in a gentle caress, sending shivers up and down her body. Goose bumps broke out where he touched her, even though the night was warm.

He pushed at her shirt and she reached down to strip it off her body without ceremony, dumping it on the floor next to her. She had never gotten used to wearing a bra, as they were not in fashion before she had been cursed, and did not do so now. Asher's eyes glittered at her naked breasts bobbing for his attention.

"That feels nice," she whispered when he put his hands on her breasts, molding them. He squeezed the flesh and then ran his thumbs over her erect nipples. Euryale gasped at the sensation and arched against his hands. His caress was soft and gentle, but she sensed the driving urgency behind his touch, and it matched the need inside her. She could not remember ever desiring a man like this, with a power that transcended everything else.

"So good," she whispered and then lay on him again, after pulling on his shirt so she could touch him skin to skin. It bunched around his shoulders in a pool of black cloth. Euryale kissed his mouth, his cheek, his jawbone and then higher, nipping at his earlobe and nuzzling his neck. He smelled musky and male. She slid his shirt over his head. Then she breathed hot air into his ear, and he trembled.

"I want to see all of you." He urged her off him and plucked at the tab of the zipper on his jeans. Euryale rolled away and made short work of her clothing, shoving it into a pile. She watched as his tanned skin was revealed as he, too, divested himself of his jeans in haste, stepping out of them and almost getting tangled up in the legs.

She would have laughed but her attention was riveted by his proud manhood, thick and erect, pointing toward her.

He gripped her and eased her back down onto the bed, kissing her as he aligned his body with hers. It was his turn to kiss her neck, her chin and then move down. As he did so, he bumped his feet against the wall in this tiny hotel room, and she laughed.

"My seduction plans are foiled by this tiny room," he muttered as he caressed her breasts again, sending her nipples into peaks of agonizing need. She gasped and gripped his naked butt, pressing her fingers into the globes. For a moment, she regretted the minuscule room and wished for a cave to linger over him, with its walls and echoes. She could hear their cries of passion doubled back to them as though they were in that stone space.

"I don't need seduction; I just need you. Asher, I ache for you. We will find time for a big room and seduction another time. Right now, I need you. Only you."

He gave her a startled glance and she wondered if she'd said too much. She pressed at his ass again, feeling his cock slide along her belly, and she reached between their bodies to caress him. He gulped and obeyed her silent command, finding the wetness between her legs and opening her folds for him. Euryale clutched at Asher and the bed shifted, creaking in the room. She moved her legs as much as she was able, and he found and pressed on her clitoris before circling it as he had done with her nipple's moments before. Her vision went white with need.

"Oh, god, Elexis, you feel so good."

"Euryale," she gasped. It was important for him to call her by her given name. She had no time to examine that feeling before his finger was sliding into her dampness while his thumb still circled her. She moaned and cried out, her orgasm a tantalizing breath away and then she was tumbling over. The sensation was so strong it was like a jolt of electricity, and then as she was still climaxing, he entered her with one sure stroke, filling her all the way to his root. He was big and thick, and she welcomed the invasion. His claiming sent silvery shockwaves over her nerve endings. His chest rubbed against her with delightful friction, sending sensation rocketing again. She gripped at his back and he kissed her, tongue clashing with hers in a welcome duel. She felt him pulsing, pulsing and his jaw clenched. He made low sounds: guttural ones wrenched from the core of him.

"Ah...Euryale...ah…" he groaned and then lifted his head, his dark hair falling around his neck and he cried out, muscles straining, and hands clasped in her hair. He went rigid, his cock thick and Euryale came again, in shivery sensations rippling through her like waves in the deep ocean, filling her and cascading through her as he climaxed, his seed spilling inside her in bursts of warmth.

As their bodies cooled, she kept her legs wrapped around him, feeling his cock still inside her. She could stay there forever.

* * *

The sun was glinting off the white marble of the Parthenon when Asher woke. Sometime during the night, Elexis…Euryale had retreated to the other tiny bed and was sprawled out, face up, snoring. It was an inelegant pose with her arms and legs akimbo, and it warmed him. She had been everything he searched for in a lover, passionate, adventurous, and talented, driving him to orgasm twice more. After their first coupling, their next bout was slower, and if possible, more intense.

She knew what she liked and how to get it. He had never met someone like her… but then again, he'd never met a goddess-turned-monster, turned back to deity in his life. It wasn't something that happened to humans.

The room was too little to stir without disturbing her, but he had to pee. He eased out of the bed as quietly as he could, considering his size and the smallness of the room, and padded to the tiny bathroom.

When he went back into the other room, she was stirring, smacking her lips together. She focused on him for a moment and her cheeks colored. He grinned at that. He relished lovers who enjoyed pleasure and didn't flinch at taking it. He had found that most women who were part of the supernatural world were not shy about sex. They had lived too long and perceived too much to let the morality of humanity rule them. Euryale was no different.

"Morning," he said with a grin. She waved at him and muttered something in return. She was *not* a morning person, and their body clocks had been thrown off by the frequent changes in location.

She said something else that was unintelligible, and he crossed the room to kiss her on the top of her head. He waited for her reaction. Their relationship was unformed and undefined, and he had no idea where they would go from here. He couldn't worry about that today, not with the sun glinting off one of the most fabulous ruins in the world and a gorgeous woman in the room with him.

"Coffee," she said and rose, dislodging the thin blanket which tumbled to the floor. She was naked, but he wasn't up to any morning nookie. Their last bout had been just a few hours before and he wasn't quite recovered. Instead he took her into his arms and held her in an undemanding embrace, feeling her warmth and her skin against his.

"Let's go down to that café we discovered yesterday. It should have a view of the Parthenon. Then we can plan our day."

She stirred and met his gaze. He didn't think there was anything more beautiful than a sleepy, naked woman against him…except maybe that same woman in the throes of orgasm, thrashing on top of him, giving her body and soul to him for those brief, ecstatic moments.

"I was around when the Parthenon was new," she said and pressed a kiss to his lips. "It was a marvel, the likes of which you will never understand. It shone in the sun for miles in every direction. The statues were gorgeous, all of them, even the one of Athena, and those who came to the Parthenon gasped when they beheld them. I wish you could have observed it then, Asher. This poor ruin does not begin to show what it was back in those days."

"I wish I could have, too. I wish there were many things I could've changed, but I wasn't around back then." The weight of years pressed down on him, but he pushed the feeling away. "I'm here now, though, so what do you say we try to get something to eat? The acrobatics last night worked up quite an appetite. I hope that café serves American breakfasts and not some continental nonsense. I need something besides a meager scrap of pastry. If they don't have it, I will…eat a horse, perhaps."

A cloud darkened her expression. "Horses can be tasty but it's a last resort. They're too useful to turn into meat. Without them, Western civilization would have had a very different outcome. It was domesticating horses that allowed humans to reach places they wouldn't have been able to get to on foot and dominate wide swathes of land. It's part of the reason the Spanish defeated South America."

He nodded. "Yeah. I've had some time to absorb history from a different point of view. I may not be your age, but I've had a few years to learn."

This time, she did smile. "Hope you like older women, Asher."

He kissed her nose. "Damn right. I always have."

* * *

The prickle in the back of her neck told Euryale a paranormal lurked nearby.

She turned to Asher and slid her arm around his waist. His warmth caused goose bumps to rise on her arms.

"Do you feel it?" she whispered.

They were in the Agora, exploring the ruins of the still-majestic site. Euryale remembered this place in its glory, just as she had the Parthenon, and the tumbled rocks and faded frescos were stark reminders of just how much time had passed when she was in her other form. Time had wrought its work on this place, but she was still the same. It was startling to think that she and her sisters had once been to this place when it was vibrant and alive. It was gone, and yet, she was still here.

"I do feel it," he said, cupping his hand to whisper in her ear. "I can't pinpoint it."

She gestured toward the city streets. "It's back toward Athens."

"Is it our enemies? Are the bastards coming at us again?" Asher spun around, checking for their foes behind them.

They had not attacked again that night, or the next day. Euryale wasn't sure what to make of what had happened. They might be playing some sort of cat and mouse game, or perhaps their energy had been depleted after strikes and needed to recharge.

"I don't believe so," she said with a shake of her head. "This feels friendlier. Come. Let's find out who is trying to get us to check on them."

He let out a breath, his face widening in alarm. "Isn't that what they want us to do? It may be minions working for whoever is doing this."

Her smirk held a glint of mischief. "Then we give them what they want. We can handle a few underlings."

He gave her a quick nod of his head. "Right you are, Ele…Euryale. Let's go." He slid his hand into hers, and together, they walked down the large stone stairs of the Agora and back to the bustling city streets of the metropolis. This was not the Athens she remembered. This was dense with traffic and pedestrians all packed together like fish in a can. The buildings tumbled over each other in loud profusion, and every inch of the square footage of the ancient city was used. In her day, Athens was the center of her world, but she could never have anticipated the sheer breadth of the number of people crammed into this place.

Asher gave her a questioning glance and she pointed toward the back side of the Agora. It was out of the way of the denser traffic of the tourists, a bit dusty and forgotten. At first reluctant, Asher then nodded.

"Goddess knows best," he said and walked on the outside of the cracked sidewalk as they made their way into the area.

A young woman, appearing to be no more than sixteen, bounced up to them.

"Can you spare a drachma?" she said and held out her hand.

She is more than she appears. Euryale kept her gaze on the teenager as she mentally spoke to Asher.

She looks like a kid.

Wait.

Euryale stepped forward and ignored the outstretched hand. The teenager continued to hold it out, assuming an aggressive stance. Her unlined face shone with the dewy blush of youth, at odds with her baseball cap and skin-tight jeans. She was wearing a T-shirt that said, "I'm not yelling, I'm Greek" and last year's trendy sneakers were on her feet. There were plenty of roaming teens in this part of the world, and many would try and steal your purse.

She was sure this one would not mind stealing a purse. Minor gods didn't change their appearance as often as the major gods liked to; it wasn't as easy for them, but this one did. The face was familiar, and welcome.

"Hebe, don't you get enough coins from Roman boys putting on their togas for the first time?"

The goddess Hebe shook her head. "That's Juvenita, the bitch, my so-called counterpart, and she doesn't share. Even though she stole her name from me, she keeps those coins for herself. She's got a superiority complex about being *Roman* and the *Romans* are so much better than the Greeks, she says. Besides, not that many Romans wear togas anymore."

"I bet you could clean up at Halloween."

Euryale struggled to contain her amusement, aware that Asher didn't have a clue what was going on.

Hebe shot Asher a disgusted glance. "Halloween is for tourists, although the bars do throw a heck of a party to separate them from their money. Apokries is our holiday, as you're aware, Gorgon, and that's in February. Even so, they dress up in the Roman style, like Romans, and I don't get a dime."

"I don't understand," Asher said, wiping his brow.

"Hebe, it's been a long time." Euryale held out her hand, and the goddess's face burst into a wide grin.

"Nice to catch up with you, Gorgon. You're a damn sight better than the last time I laid eyes on you."

"You too," Euryale said. "Asher, this is Hebe. She is married to the demigod, Heracles."

Hebe waved a hand. "Old news. That bastard is out chasing young tail. I got rid of him centuries ago. Do you go by Elexis or Euryale now?"

Euryale considered. Going by Elexis was supposed to make her comfortable, but it was the opposite. Regardless of how hard she had tried to think of herself as Elexis, she was Euryale. It was impossible not to in this land, where she was born and raised, until becoming a monster.

"Elexis for most, but you can call me Euryale," she said. "This is Asher."

"One of Clíodhna's," Hebe said and eyed Asher with every appearance of measuring him for temple duties. "Not bad, if you like the type."

Asher shook Hebe's hand. "You don't appear to be much like a goddess. I'm afraid my comprehension of Greek gods is a bit rusty, current crash course notwithstanding."

Hebe chewed on some gum and then spat it out into the gutter. For a moment the image shimmered, and a slender figure stood before them wearing a sleeveless long dress in a simple drape style. Then the image faded, and she was the young woman again with her sneakers and T-shirt.

"That's what you get being the goddess of youth," she said with a grin. "It's such a bother these days. Kids grow up so fast, all that crap."

They were speaking in English, Hebe having the faintest hint of an accent. Once upon a time they had been friends, even after Euryale's transition. For a while, anyway. All things faded in the fullness of time.

"Isn't that what all parents say?" Asher interjected and gestured to the T-shirt.

"Good advice."

Hebe examined her T-shirt and her mouth twisted. "I like to warn people. You Americans get so offended."

Euryale didn't recall the youthful goddess being so cranky.

"It must be hard to stay feeling young when you've been alive for centuries," Asher commented, and again there was a twinkle in his eye.

"Shut it, banshee," Hebe snapped. "I don't draw baths for your father anymore, and I'm not doing it for you." She grinned at Asher. "I like you. You've got style, for a demigod. Come on. Let's get some grub. I want to talk to you."

Chapter Eleven

A high-pitched keening sound broke their conversation. As one, the three turned to face the source of the noise. Windows of the building next to them shattered, raining glass down toward the street. The repeat of the night before did not elude Asher.

Euryale began running and Hebe and Asher followed. Euryale was faster than anything he'd witnessed in his hundred years of life. The racket echoed off the other buildings as they raced back toward the Parthenon. The young goddess called Hebe ran behind them, trying to keep the pace. She didn't appear to be someone who would get involved with their problem, but maybe he was just judging her on her aspect. If he didn't recognize she was an immortal goddess, he would have believed her to be fifteen.

What are you doing? He shot the question into Euryale's mind. They were moving so fast people were still beginning to react to the noise. Some were pointing, and those who'd been in the five-story building were poking their heads out from the now-empty windows, looking down to the street below.

It's the same mental signature as last night. Can't you feel it? They are playing with us. I don't like being toyed with.

There was another boom, like a sonic scream across their senses. Asher's ears rang in the aftermath. Euryale vaulted up the steps of the Parthenon, almost knocking over slower tourists in her haste. Asher and Hebe followed behind, slower than the woman leaping four steps at a time.

Asher marveled at Euryale's stamina. She didn't tire. Neither did Hebe. The same couldn't be said for him. He was in excellent shape, but he couldn't keep up this pace for very long.

They continued up the stone steps of the Parthenon until they reached the top. The guards shouted at them as they ran past the ticket booth, but Euryale went through without slowing, Asher and Hebe behind. The sonic boom came again, echoing and shaking the stones of the monument. Euryale sprinted to the back of the structure and then glanced at the other two. Down below them on the hills were more stones, and an amphitheater that showed the dark spots and weathered air of something very old.

"I think they're that way."

Hebe grinned. "Let's go." She led the way, plummeting over the grass and down the hill, making impossible leaps to get to the arrangement that looked closer than it was. They followed, the shouts of the humans fading behind them. Within moments, they were in the old stone circular area. Asher's gaze went from the cracked stones to the pattern, and then to the hill that the old meeting place was cut into. The Parthenon loomed above them. Down here it was quiet.

They waited for what seemed to be a long time, but there was no activity in the old ruin. He peered at Euryale.

She clenched her fists and shook her head. "I thought they were here."

"It's empty," he said, his voice resonating in the space.

Euryale raised her head to the sky. Then she cried out, the sound piercing the air. It echoed off the hills around them, bouncing around like they were in an echo chamber. Hebe flinched and covered her ears, and Asher winced. He stared at Euryale in amazement. His banshee side yearned to join in with her, to add his voice to hers, and shatter the peaks with their combined cries.

When she stopped, Hebe snorted indelicately and shook her head. "Feel better?" she asked with a wry, knowing smile that gave her youthful countenance an older appearance.

"Not really," Euryale said. "It confirms my suspicions, though."

A multitude of rocks that had been loosened by time tumbled into the ancient amphitheater, their fall adding to the tableau.

"They have sound power, Asher. Why else would the Gorgon, famous for her bellowing cries, and a half banshee be tasked for this mission? Otherwise the gods wouldn't have bothered with us. I wager Ares had different plans for your promise to him, and I doubt Athena had any interest in converting me and my sisters back into women. It was expedient for her to do so, but she took no pleasure in it."

"I wouldn't take that bet if I were you, handsome. Euryale knows what she's talking about," Hebe said, and Asher shot her a glance.

"Handsome?" Euryale swatted at Hebe, who dodged out of her way. "Don't get your mitts anywhere near him. This one is mine."

Hebe tilted back against the rough stone of the ancient monument. "Is that right? I was married to Heracles, remember? I get it about demigods and heroes. You're out of practice."

For a moment, it appeared that Euryale was going to smack Hebe, but to his surprise, she studied the other woman for several moments before reaching over and hugging her. He was shocked by the easy intimacy. Euryale wasn't one who touched others, but she'd just looped her arms around the other woman like they'd been friends for centuries.

Which, of course, they had been. It was hard to keep up sometimes.

"Thanks, you pain in the ass," Euryale said.

"I liked you better as a monster," Hebe said without heat and then turned to Asher.

"Come on. Time for lunch. I'm sure you have a lot of questions, and we should get out of here before the Greek police come and haul us off for being where we're not supposed to be."

* * *

"You used to visit her?"

Euryale wasn't sure she liked that open-mouthed shock on Asher's face. It reminded her of the times she'd been a monster and people recoiled. Hebe was always inclined to do things others didn't just for the sheer pleasure of rebelling. It was part of who she was.

Hebe ran her straw around the inside of her glass of *portokalada*, releasing the condensation. The popular Greek soft drinks hadn't existed when she'd left the country for the last time.

"Yea, so what?" Hebe said with a snarl that would not have been out of place on a muscled bouncer. The other woman may have the face and body of a fifteen-year-old, but she was as ancient as Euryale, and as interested in the opposite sex.

Asher took a sip of his *vissinada*, a kind of sour cherry soda that Euryale was also imbibing and shot Hebe a neutral appraisal. Euryale appreciated that lack of interest—a lot.

The outdoor café was off the main thoroughfare, but plenty of people walked by and the tables were almost filled. Euryale didn't like anything about the crush of the city, not the people, not the cars, not the subway cars, and not the way Hebe was studying Asher as though she'd like to find out how a tall banshee and a diminutive goddess fit together.

The jealousy that spiked through Euryale was as green as her skin had once been, and as ill-fitting. Even as she bore it, she recognized the absurdity of the emotion. Hebe may have the appearance of a child, but she had always been a friend. If Asher tried to date her, that was between Hebe and Asher. It wasn't up to Euryale to lead Asher's life for him.

"So nothing," Asher said. "It's just that I got the impression nobody would talk to the Gorgons, least of all the gods."

"I'm not good at doing what I'm supposed to be," Hebe replied with a studied indifference that Euryale was aware hid a lot of past hurts. "People don't take me seriously anyway, so I do what I want, and fuck them."

He grinned and Euryale's heart turned over.

"Good attitude," he said. "Can I ask you a question and you won't take offense?"

Hebe glared at him and then shifted her attention to Euryale. "It's a good thing your boyfriend is cute because he's impudent. Asher, you don't ask goddesses questions like that. Some, like the vain, pretty ones, might think you're going to ask them about wrinkles and smite you."

He raised his hands. "I don't have to ask if you don't want to answer."

"Until I hear the question, I can't tell you if I will answer or not."

Euryale expected him to ask something about her and was surprised by his next question. "How badly does it suck to be stuck in the body of a kid? Do you always get carded? Or do you tell them to fuck off?"

Instead of answering, Hebe's visage altered. Not enough to make her unrecognizable, but her face filled into more mature lines, adding depth and maturity to her countenance that made her more like twenty-five and not the fifteen of her original face.

Asher nodded. "Got it. You're a goddess. Dumb question."

Hebe shifted back to her youthful face. "This is who I am, and most of the time, I couldn't care less what people think. People also don't give kids the same kind of drama they give adults, so I get away with more. The creeps who like underage women get on my nerves, though. I've helped the cops catch a few in my day."

Hebe tapped the table. "The Gorgons were given a raw deal. Athena can be a raving bitch. There was no reason for any of them to pay for Poseidon getting his rocks off, but old Athy couldn't handle the fact that her temple maiden was no wilting flower." She studied Euryale. "If you guys hadn't backed her up, you might have come through it okay."

Euryale picked up her *vissinada*, which was the color of hibiscus, and took a long drink. "Sisters don't abandon sisters."

"And friends don't abandon friends."

Yes, many would underestimate Hebe, and by all accounts, Asher had been one of those people. Her handsome—*lover?*—was studying the other goddess with a speculative gaze.

"What? I have dirt on my nose?"

Hebe must have been spending time in America because she talked like an American teen. Or maybe that was how the Greek kids spoke these days.

"No, you just surprised me, that's all. I didn't think Euryale had any friends. The myths made it appear the monsters were alone." He glanced at Euryale. "I'm glad you weren't without help."

Her heart stopped and then sped up. A glow spread throughout Euryale, one of belonging and well-being. She had no business feeling this way or even thinking of Asher as anything other than a fling. They would solve this mystery, stop the god killers, and then go their separate ways. They had been brought together by circumstance and not by choice. There would be no future for a Gorgon and a banshee.

No matter how much she might want it.

* * *

Euryale was a goddess and a monster. She was a woman without friends and yet she had people who helped her. She claimed to be powerless, but she had a heck of a lot of influence. She was in every way a delicious contradiction.

"We need to get out of Athens. The answers aren't in this city."

She was lying across the narrow bed, an alluring sight, wearing nothing but air and the touch of a sheet draped across her midsection. It did little to hide her body, and his cock rose in response to her state of semi-nudity.

"We were attacked here," he pointed out, trailing a hand over the curve of her waist before resting it on her thigh. Not for Euryale was the trimmed and coiffed pubic hair of modern times, she had pubic hair that reminded him of seventies porn stars. It was a throwback to his early days as well, when women didn't wax and shave their nether regions until they screamed.

"Those were games. There's too much chatter here. Our perpetrators won't get far in Athens."

He frowned again. "Isn't this where the gods are?"

Euryale shook her head with a weary air. "Not at this time. Mount Olympus doesn't have a fixed location in the world, per se, except that it is in Greece. It's part of the mythology, so here it stays. "It's near Thessaloniki at the moment. These people—whoever they are—aren't going to attack the gods in their kingdom. They're going to pick off the weaker ones outside Olympus."

"Weaker ones like your friend Hebe? Has she put herself in danger?"

Euryale shifted away from him, a movement he couldn't tell whether it was indifference or trying to conceal a greater emotion. "I'll figure out a way to make sure she is okay. It's us they're after now that we've set things in motion. We've got to find out who this is, and who they might be aiming for next."

He trailed a hand over her thigh, and she shivered.

"We have to come up with a better plan, Euryale. We've been following their trail, but we don't have a plan for what we do when, or if we find them."

"We've come this far without knowing what to do. Let's get some paper so we can write this out."

Asher stared at her for a few moments and then laughed. In response, he grabbed his tablet off the coffee table and turned it on.

"We don't need paper, goddess. We've got everything we need right here."

She scowled at him. "I think better when I write stuff down."

"Try this first. If it doesn't work, I'll get you more paper."

Her mouth opened to argue with him but then she shut it and nodded.

"Okay. We'll do it your way. I guess this way we can redo it again and again without wasting precious resources."

"That's right, oh goddess. I'm glad that you can change your ways. It shows flexibility of mind."

She growled, showing her teeth in a way that made him hard.

"You want flexible? I'll show you flexible."

It was many hours before they got back to the plan. First, he kissed her until they were breathless, and then he caressed her until she cried out and clung to him. He could almost detect the snakes in her hair. Then she was all soft, warm Euryale, a goddess and a lover who stirred his senses. As he entered her, their bodies slick with passion, he understood that something had changed with them, something that could change his life if he let it.

He lost himself to his orgasm, hearing her cry out with the same satisfaction, and wondered what would happen next.

Chapter Twelve

"Why are we going to a museum?"

There was such pique in Asher's voice that it quavered and would have sounded like a cranky old man if not for the strength in its resonant tones.

"The National Archaeological Museum wasn't here when I was last in Athens, and I'm curious," she said. "I want to consult with the museum and find out how they got it wrong."

He ran his hand over her back, and she shivered. She expected to be uncomfortable with public displays of affection, but this was Asher, and she didn't mind.

"It's a waste of time. Shouldn't we be going to the Plaka to parade around like we did the other night, or take the subway to draw their attention? A museum is full of dull, boring artifacts."

"The museum is full of things that are part of my history," she said.

Asher frowned for several more moments and then his face brightened. "That's right. I'll learn about you. Let's go. Do they have Gorgons?"

"I am sure they do."

She showed him the website as they walked through the dense traffic of Athens and began reading aloud. "The National Archaeological Museum in Athens is the largest of its kind in Greece and one of the most important museums in the world devoted to Greek art. It was founded to house and protect antiquities from all over Greece, thus displaying their historical, cultural, and artistic value. Although its original purpose was to secure all the finds from the nineteenth century excavations in and around Athens, it became the central National

Archaeological Museum and was enriched with finds from all over Greece. Its abundant collections, with more than 11,000 exhibits, provide a panorama of Greek civilization from the beginnings of Prehistory to Late Antiquity."

She finished and gazed at Asher.

"Sounds like a ton of laughs," Asher grumbled, and she laughed, her spirit lighter than it had a right to be with all the things pressing down on them.

"Asher, you didn't even have a dad or a granddad to show you how to be a grumpy old guy. That's for humans. What's wrong?"

He sighed and slung an arm around her. "It's not the museum," he admitted. "It's everything. We're just shooting in the dark. I would do anything not to continue this quest, but…" He stopped in the middle of the Plaka and people started flowing around them, casting them dirty looks.

"I don't want you getting hurt," he continued, the sincerity on his face leaving her no doubt that he meant every word. "I don't want you mixed up in this. It's too dangerous. You should leave. Go someplace where that bitch Athena can't find you and hide out. Let me take care of this. I don't want anything to happen to you."

There were so many people who had never tried to help her. She and Stheno had been each other's only source of strength for centuries. She recalled the loneliness, and the weight of all those years made her stagger.

"Asher, that isn't possible," she said, kissing him before urging him to start walking again. "First of all, the answer is no. There isn't anywhere on this planet where the gods can't find us. That is a fantasy. It may take Athena time but even in other pantheons' underworlds, she could locate me if she put her mind to it. If I betrayed this promise, that would be the least of it. She would hunt my sisters, too, and Medusa is vulnerable. I am not the running type. You have to realize that by now."

"Yeah," he said and pointed to the street when they resumed their pace. "I do get that. But this thing kills gods and I…I don't want you to die."

Her heart did a funny flip and started hammering in her chest. It was pointless to speculate on everything that Asher meant behind his words. All those years she had been unlovable and now she was restored. That might not be enough.

"Asher, are you forgetting that if you abandon this quest your life is forfeit? Possibly your mother's as well. That's what the gods do. They make it impossible for you to refuse. Even if you were to sacrifice yourself, she would be at risk. No, Asher. We both made promises and we will both keep our word. There are gods who go after those who are false and oath breakers. If we went back on our word, Athena might not have to do her dirty work. She could send Adrestia."

"Great. More gods."

The museum was located a short distance from the Acropolis, an easy walk even through the dense crowd. After getting directions from a local shopkeeper, who tried to sell them Greece-themed trinkets, they walked to the museum.

The outside was almost as impressive as the Acropolis, which it might have been modeled after. The front was white, with columns holding up the edifice that led to the inside. People streamed up and down the white stairs in a steady flow.

They paid their admission fee and went to the first room. When they entered, there was a vestibule staircase, leading up to the next level with people covering it going both directions. All around her was the feel of her ancestry in the marbles and the promise of antiquities in the spacious place.

"Where to first? Prehistoric collection or Mycenaean?" Asher asked, taking her hand and swinging their clasped hands between them like a metronome. There was something brittle about him, like her reminder of his own Sword of Damocles had shifted his insides.

"The Gorgons didn't exist during the Mycenaean era, so perhaps that one," she said and was awarded with a surprised stare from Asher.

"What do you mean?"

"It's complicated with gods," she said as they wandered over to the section that had antiquities dating back into the fifteenth century BC. "Humans have to believe in us for us to exist. When they do, we are everything they think we are: immortal, unchanging, with all the qualities they bestow upon us. If the Romans had managed to take us over one hundred percent and push us into oblivion, we would fade away. It's complicated, as I said."

He studied a plaster head of a woman, and she read the inscription. It was a goddess or a sphinx, an example of monumental Mycenaean plastic art.

The placard read: From the area of the Cult Centre on the acropolis at Mycenae from 13th century BC.

"The facial features, with their severe expression, are accentuated by touches of bright red-and-black paint, while dotted rosettes brighten up the cheeks and chin. The hair falls in small curls along the forehead."

She turned to Asher. "That deity predates us. Nobody worships her anymore. She has been forgotten. That is how it goes with gods."

He gave her a thoughtful glance. "Can you please explain it to me once and for all? If nobody believes in you, you fade away?"

She nodded. "That's right. A few centuries ago, the god Ashur from Ashurism tried to cling to power long after his time had passed. Last time people saw him, he was a shade. He must be gone by now. That's why whoever is doing this started with minor pantheons. If only a few go missing, it's natural to think that they vanished due to lack of belief. The opposite is true of the Greek, Roman, Egyptian, and Norse pantheons. Many people believe in them. Pantheons like the Albanians are lesser, and therefore have less influence."

"I've never understood this, although it's what I've been told is true. It always felt like a fairy tale and I've never given it much credence. You're gods. If people stopped believing in the Greek myths, you'd fade away?"

"Over time. It wouldn't happen for quite a while. Humanity would have to stop and then we would fade. That's much harder to do in a world of electronic media. But for all the supernatural beings who say the world would be better off without humans, they don't consider the cost. Or they don't believe it."

He shook his head and viewed another piece of ancient sculpture.

"Then the gods should want to preserve humanity instead of being so capricious with it," he said as they moved to the next display.

"You forget their arrogance."

They wandered through the early-and-middle-age Bronze Era sculptures and other marvels. Asher was quiet.

They dodged people leaving the Egyptian collection. She tilted an eyebrow at Asher, and he nodded to the statuary visible beyond.

"I'd like to see their representation of Gorgons," he replied, and Euryale shook her head.

"I'd rather not."

He took her hand. "They're statues. They can't hurt you."

"I have made many statues in my time," she said, nonetheless allowing herself to be led.

The first head that they found was cast in stone and featured a woman's head with a grotesque appearance, her tongue sticking out. Euryale grimaced but said nothing. Next they stopped in front of a tall vase protected behind glass, which the description said was a funerary amphora, that described in red, black, and tan drawings—the beheading of Medusa. A tour group buzzed up behind them, the teacher droning on.

"This is the myth of Perseus, who beheaded the Gorgon, Medusa. He was given a shield to detect her by and the gift of invisibility to protect him."

Euryale stiffened and tried to drown out the words by low humming. This had been a mistake. She fought the urge to turn and bare her teeth at the teacher lecturing his students about the old myth.

"Can anyone tell me why Perseus was able to kill Medusa?"

The children shuffled their feet, a study in boredom. Finally, one spoke.

"Is he like Percy Jackson?"

The teacher frowned. "That is not the lesson. Anyone else?"

A girl raised her hand. "Perseus used the shield Athena had given him to find Medusa without looking at her and cut off her head that way. Then he escaped the wrath of her two sisters by becoming invisible using the hat of darkness."

"Very good," the teacher said. "And then?"

Euryale turned away from the lesson.

Are you okay?

It's hard to hear, even after all this time. The myth is so pervasive, I almost believe it.

His hand slid into hers and she accepted his touch. She had never met a man who took her just as she was, without asking her to be something else. Not even when she had been a goddess.

Of course, he had never beheld her monster side. She had no doubt that he would shun her if he watched snakes coil around her face, and took in her green hide, scales, claws, and tail.

"Why did Athena both turn Medusa and the Gorgons, and then also give Perseus a shield to defeat you? Didn't she want you to suffer?"

Euryale turned her face to his, unable to stop the tears piercing her cheeks.

"That's the gods for you," she said. "Athena doesn't think she is in the wrong. Medusa lost her virginity in Athena's temple, and therefore she had to pay. Giving Perseus the tools to kill her was just one more way that the gods show how little they care about us."

He paused and she waited.

"How…how did Medusa survive? You said that all your sisters were changed back as a condition of helping the gods, but Medusa had her head cut off. The legend says that Perseus dripped blood in his flight back and created snakes. It said he used the head to turn Phineas to stone. But your sister is…alive, isn't she? You don't refer to her as dead."

Euryale grinned at him with private satisfaction. "Medusa's head *was* cut off, but we reattached it. The legend does not tell that part. Mythology is always much more interesting than the actual tale. Perseus did kill her, but even though Medusa was mortal in her natural life, she became a creature in her monsterhood and that helped us to bring her back to life. Medusa retained her frailness and cannot be awake for long periods. She is in a cave in the wild country of Sumeria, in what is now Iraq. We paid a local enchanter to spell the cave so she could remain undisturbed. Stheno has undertaken to go there to determine her status now that we have our human appearance again. It is a question we will need to answer once this is done. Of the three of us, my sister is the most vulnerable."

They turned to go, and the room shook.

* * *

The kids, who were still gathered around the vase bearing the paintings of the killing of Medusa, screamed. Asher's gaze shifted from where Euryale was still gazing at the vase with a sorrowful air, to the children, and back toward the doorway.

"Earthquake," someone shouted even as the statues rocked. The floor bucked beneath their feet, but Asher was used to earthquakes. The panicked visitors started to flee while the room groaned.

There was something odd about the vibration, though. Asher knew from experience that you heard a quake beforehand much of the time. He had detected nothing. He glanced at Euryale. Her attention was riveted to a space beyond the door.

"This isn't a quake, is it?"

She opened her mouth in a motion reminiscent of the snakes she no longer bore.

"No," she said. The statuary, which must have been bolted in place, rocked again, but nothing was in danger of falling over. In the distance, security shouted in both Greek and English for people to evacuate. In this earthquake-prone country area, they had been trained in what to do. The shouting went on as the room shook yet again and Euryale's attention shifted for a second time. A moment later, he felt a tug toward the next room where her gaze had landed.

"That way, I take it?"

They dodged behind a statue as a security guy came to check the room and then darted to the next room where there was an almost invisible door in the wall. She pushed against it and Asher was unsurprised that it was unlocked. The room quavered again but there was no rolling aftermath, just an intermittent shaking. Anyone with experience of quakes would recognize this was unnatural.

"Something is causing this," he said.

"Yes, and it has help." She cocked her head. The din was too loud, the confusion rampant as voices intermingled, some shouting over the others. He had a mental image of people running from place to place with no clear direction in mind, like sheep driven mad with terror. "Listen to them. Even taking into account tourists and their fear of quakes, there is mass confusion. They are being compelled." She stepped inside and closed the door behind them.

"What's going on?"

"We're about to find out."

Out of nowhere, several shrieking figures came lunging at them, hands raised like claws. They sped toward the duo with lightning speed, much faster than they should have been able to. Asher could make no sense of things.

"Run," Euryale said. They darted around a corner, but their pursuers didn't follow. The hallway they stepped into was quiet, although the noise of the fleeing mob of people was clear even in this space. They closed the door behind them, and Asher took a deep breath, his body tensing for battle.

Asher was about to breathe out a sigh of relief but something else came at them. They were oddly shaped and appeared inhuman, more like…

"Dwarves?" Asher asked as a pair of beings charged toward them. They weren't even five-feet high and had the aspect of monkeys in face and body, although their limbs were human. They dove for Asher and Euryale.

"*Kerkopes,*" Euryale panted, wrestling with the nearest creature. His teeth clacked as he tried to bite her face. She pushed at him and he tumbled to the ground. He leaped back up and went for her again. Asher was engaged in a fistfight with his smaller combatant, who was holding his own against the larger man.

There was a booming sound and the *Kerkopes* turned and fled.

"Explain," Asher managed when the boom faded.

"They are from the legend of Heracles," she said. "They were thieves, but they amused him, so he spared their lives. That would have been fine except they pissed off Zeus, so he turned them into monkeys. They are the sons of Oceanus, a Titan, by Theia, who was a mortal daughter of the king, Memnon."

"Why is someone sending random creatures to attack us?"

She opened her mouth to answer but another boom and a thud echoed around them. Even the dust shivered in this space.

"What now?" Asher groaned as they fled deeper into the bowels of the museum. It was darker here, lit by occasional lamps.

"We're about to find out."

A gigantic fox appeared in front of them.

"The *Alopex Teumesios*," she said and gestured to him to circle behind the beast. "It's a fox which ravaged the kingdom of Thebes, preying upon the children of the country."

"Shouldn't it be dead?" He gaped at the red-masked intruder, who hissed at them.

"Dead or alive, it's going to swat you if you don't duck right now."

Asher dipped, and the fox's paw swung right over him.

"Bring it on, asshole," Asher said, shaking a fist at the fox, who stared at him from his enormous height.

"Asher, we have to get out of here. The artifacts housed in this place are precious to me and I would not want them harmed. They are all we have of our history."

He nodded and scanned the area.

"Back the way we came?"

A moment later, Asher and Euryale were rushing back through the rooms and joining the humans. Security frowned at them and peered back at the deserted room but made no comment. They continued running down the white steps and into the bright afternoon sunshine.

They came to a halt a block away and he fell into step behind Euryale. She kept moving away from the building, putting distance between them and the museum.

"I guess they don't have a love of history," Asher said. Euryale still said nothing, casting a speculative glance back before turning her gaze to the Parthenon, and stopping.

"I'm not sure you are correct. They didn't destroy anything. In fact, they waited until we were in that deserted area of the museum to throw their creatures at us. They tried not to destroy the antiquities. The people we are pursuing are Greek. I am confident of that, after today's incident, coupled with what's happened over the last few days."

"I agree. It only makes sense. What was it about what happened in there that makes you so certain?"

She pointed toward the building high up on the hill. "When we were in Los Angeles, we detected them, but they were far away. We didn't feel them in Ireland or Albania, and any residual effects of their attack in Albania were long gone. Since we arrived here, the attacks have become more frequent and violent. They led us here." She paused. "Those creatures they sent to us were obscure. Greeks would have read about them, but nobody else. Our adversaries are taunting us, daring us to find them. They have set down a series of clues."

"They laid out breadcrumbs, and like good birds, we gobbled them up," he mused and then rubbed his hand over his chin. "I agree with you. What does that mean?"

"It means we're in the right place. It means that the plan we are working on needs to be finished and put into motion."

She turned her face to his, and there was fear stamped on her features. "It means, we're in the greatest danger of our lives."

Chapter Thirteen

"What do we know about them?"

Euryale handed the tablet to Asher with a listing of the Grecian gods.

"They're Greek, as we've thought. It makes sense. The major pantheon brought us in when the danger became too great, and they hired me, one of the Gorgons, as defense. They may have been aware right from the beginning that these creatures were Greek, but until it affected them, they didn't care. When the danger didn't dissipate, Athena acted. I hate that woman."

There were so many things he could say, but Asher contented himself with nodding. His body thrummed to take action. After their trip to the museum, Euryale hurried back to the hotel and logged onto the Internet. She spent several minutes looking things up and Asher let her be, burning with curiosity about what she was after.

She said nothing for almost a half hour, her attention going from the computer to the Parthenon. Then she sighed and pushed the device away.

"I'm missing something," she said with a groan. "There are pieces that aren't adding up. Up until now all the attacks have been remote and easy to deflect. Even the one in the museum was just a smoke screen. It wasn't our main adversaries—they don't want to show themselves. There's more. They are not here."

He frowned. "Not here in Greece?"

She shook her head. "No. They are in Greece. Whatever they are going to do, it is against the Greek pantheon. I would have said Thessaloniki, but there are too many gods around. If it were that easy, then they would have already acted. They are somewhere else. I can't get through their shields, but I'm getting a sense of them. As a monster, I was a good tracker, and I still have that ability. I think…" She paused. "I think they're *not* in Athens."

"What does that mean?"

"It means that we're not in the right part of Greece." Her head was tilted in a gesture Asher now associated with Euryale in thought.

"We need to get out of Athens. We need to go…"

Despite what she said moments before, he still expected Euryale to say Thessaloniki or one of the other urban centers. Asher waited. He was never sure what his fascinating Gorgon was going to say next.

"The islands. That is our destination. My instincts are pointing me that way. After millennia of being a creature driven on urges, I can tell you they are not wrong."

"I don't ever doubt your gut sense," he said, trying to project sincerity in his voice and in his mind. "Which one?"

She paused as she considered his question. Silence filled the room for long, uncomfortable moments. He held his breath, trying not to speak until she did. He couldn't have said why it was important not to shatter the moment.

"Crete. That's what I'm getting. However, there is too much intrusion from Athens and the gods and creatures here to be sure. We should start with Kythira. Its past is connected to Aphrodite and not Athena, so we shouldn't run into any interference from that one. I feel strongly we need to go there."

He put a hand on her shoulder. "Why would Athena interfere? She has an interest in making sure we succeed. It's her ass on the line, too."

Euryale made a face. "Yeah, but she doesn't need to make it easy for me. She hates me and nothing will change that. It is a feeling very much returned."

There was nothing to say to that.

* * *

The plane flew low over the blue Aegean, a sight that soothed Euryale's soul.

Tiny, uninhabited islands dotted the landscape. Around them the water flowed, the eternal, endless sea where Poseidon reigned. She loved the ocean but hated the god for what he had done to her sister. In the end, it was Athena who had cast them out, Athena who Medusa had prayed to for forgiveness and received a horrible curse in return. She could almost excuse Poseidon for his folly—times and gods were different back then—but she didn't like him. She didn't mind other sea gods and liked the water, but this one she could do without. Poseidon had long since moved on and would never have remembered his recklessness in Athena's temple if his wife hadn't taken such extreme revenge.

"Kythira is located between the Greek mainland and Crete. There is a temple of Aphrodite on the island and it is considered one of her places, along with Cyprus."

"Is Aphrodite as beautiful as the myths say, or is that nonsense as well?"

His question earned him a sharp glare from Euryale, and she resisted the urge to swat him. "What do you think?"

Despite it all, it stung. She didn't want to think of Asher's attention focused on another woman.

Asher tried to tug her to him, but she twisted out of reach.

"I think that Aphrodite is as stunning as Prende. I bet if I met Venus or any of the other goddesses of love, they would be the same. Gorgeous. So what? There are tons of goddesses of love. There are too many gods and too many pantheons. No matter where you go here, you're tripping over one. It gets annoying."

Euryale leveled her gaze at him. He blinked and raised a hand. There must have been some of her power in that stare, and she glanced away before any residual power surfaced. Of all the people in the world, he was one of the few she would not wish to turn to stone.

"Aphrodite is so beautiful, she is hard to observe. Why do you think the gods change their appearance? It's great to be so gorgeous that people stop and stare, but when everyone looks that way, it loses its influence. That's why some gods stay in their different forms. Beauty doesn't have the clout it has in the human world. We expect our goddesses of love to be spectacular, and others also want to be phenomenally attractive. After a while nobody cares."

"Do you have that skill?"

She tilted her head back and forth. "To an extent. I'm immortal and a goddess but I'm not from a major pantheon. If I tried, I could change my appearance, but it wouldn't last."

"Looks don't matter to me. I hated the way so many women in Los Angeles changed their face. I would rather behold the real you than some artificial face created by your god power."

She yearned to burrow against him and let him hold her. She had a brief, fanciful moment of the idea of running away with him, to someplace where the gods couldn't find her. That was impossible. You could hide from a god for a time, but immortal lives were long, and even the best hiding places were uncovered.

"What do you suggest we do when we get to Kythira?" she asked instead, wishing she had the courage to tell Asher what she was feeling. It was stupid to think that they had any sort of future, but the feelings burned in her breast, begging to be expressed.

She tapped the back of the seat. The plane was loud, and the only other passengers were two local people who appeared to be heading there for work.

"It's Aphrodite's island. We go to the temple and try to talk to Aphrodite."

* * *

He was never going to get used to this talking to gods stuff. Asher hadn't grasped how sheltered his life had been vis-à-vis the god thing until he got involved with a creature from legend. Before their recent visit, it had been a long time since he'd been in Ireland.

Kythira was drenched in sunlight, with steep, rocky hills that showed the region's propensity for earthquakes. The houses were typical of the area, most of them white, with tiled roofs and painted blue doors. He could feel the history in the myriad buildings—it was prevalent in every wall and tile.

With Euryale by his side… Perhaps it was foolish to think that a millennia-old goddess who was also a fierce monster would want to be with him. He would find out once this was over. Until then, he wasn't going to say anything. He kept his feelings locked away behind his shield.

"I've never been here," Euryale said, her hair whipping around her. He had a quick mental image of what she would be like with snakes for hair as her thick locks were buffeted by the wind. For a moment, he wondered if the snakes still lived there, hidden and sleeping but not gone.

The idea should have scared him. Instead, he found it compelling.

"Me either," he said, earning a smirk from her. He fisted his hand in her hair and tugged her toward him. He bent down to claim her lips. The kiss went on several moments longer than he intended. When he broke away from her, they were both breathless.

She slid her hand into his and he gripped it, pressing his bigger palm against hers. Her hand was a bit rough, showing the aftereffects of her years in another form, but he didn't like fragile women, anyway.

They went through the airport gates and out onto the island. There was a handful of cars around and a bus idling nearby. Asher studied the rocky terrain, blinking in the bright sunshine.

"Isn't Cyprus where Aphrodite is most associated with?"

Euryale gave him a pleased smile, like he had learned an important lesson. There was such an enigma to her—she was every inch a mysterious goddess.

"Cyprus is linked to Aphrodite, but Kythira makes a good claim. Always go beyond the fine print in myths, Asher."

"You're the boss in this. You know far more than I do. I accept that Aphrodite was part of this island. The natives think so, and if you've taught me anything, it's that belief has a hand in shaping mythology almost as much as actual fact. So, where do we go now?"

"I think we go right to the source. Aphrodite's temple is—was—in Paleokastro. The temple itself is gone, but there is a church there that the tour guides say shows the Doric columns of Aphrodite's old temple. Hebe didn't say that that was our destination, but she told us to head this way. She may be a bit of a scoundrel, but she doesn't lie."

"That sounds good. But if it's a church, why would Aphrodite show up there? If her temple was dismantled, wouldn't she be pissed?"

Euryale twirled her hand in a circular motion to indicate their surroundings. "Most of our ancient structures are gone. They were either torn down by invaders, looted for the marble, or taken down as heretical monuments and replaced by other buildings. Our culture lies in other buildings, or beneath the waves."

He frowned. "Like Atlantis?"

Euryale gave an exasperated sigh and swatted him on the arm.

"Atlantis is a myth. If you want to understand the truth behind the Atlantis legend, you have to go to the island of Santorini, which was once Thera. We live in a seismically active part of the world and accidents happen. Treasure hunters find many things in the Aegean Sea. There is much in the ocean, but that is Poseidon's domain and I don't go there. I have no interest."

"Still holding a grudge against Poseidon?"

She glared toward the ocean like the god was there. "He is an arrogant god and he did Medusa ill, but he didn't cause what happened to us. He could have stopped it, but so could many other gods. They chose not to. The major pantheon is an egotistical bunch."

"Then why are we here? Aphrodite is part of the major pantheon. Why would you want to go to her for help?"

"That is my question as well."

* * *

A woman stood in front of them, dressed in shorts and a loose-fitting sleeveless blouse. Her hair was curly and bound on top of her head.

"Hello, Euryale. Brother."

Asher slid his gaze to Euryale. She was shaking, whether with rage or anticipation, it was hard to tell. If he were honest with himself, he wasn't sure what to feel, either.

"Harmonia," Euryale said, and the two women nodded at each other. Asher searched his mind but came up with nothing. She had to be a goddess, but he had no clue who she was. She called him brother, so she was related to Ares.

"I believe you already recognize who Asher is. Asher, this is Harmonia. She is the daughter of Ares and Aphrodite, and the goddess of harmony and concord."

The woman smirked and regarded him up and down with a faint air of disdain. Not being familiar with what else to do, he held out his hand.

She ignored his hand and inclined her head to him in the manner of a queen to her subordinate.

"I repeat my question," she said, focusing back on Euryale. "Why are you here? My mother's island has little to offer you."

Asher cleared his throat. "If you're the goddess of harmony, then I would think you would understand why we're here. Someone is killing gods. They appear to be Greek. Why wouldn't you be more interested?"

She made a tsking sound. "Athena hired you to stop them. That is all I need. It's your job to do, and nothing to do with me or Mother."

He took a step forward, wanting to do…something. Euryale restrained him with a hand on his arm. He almost laughed at the idea that the famous monster was the one showing some sense.

"You're not exactly living up to your name. This quest has to do with all of us," he sputtered and earned another glare from his sister. If these were the sort of siblings he had to claim from his Greek heritage, he would stick with the banshees.

Harmonia waved a hand and let it flutter to her side before pointing in the distance.

"Come. There is a place in Chora near the Historical Archives of Kythira where she will meet us. This way."

Asher and Euryale followed.

Chapter Fourteen

That was a goddess for you. Always showing off.

The Greek goddess of love and beauty radiated sex appeal in all directions. The villagers and tourists followed her every move, their tongues practically lolling out of their mouths. She shone so bright, she was dazzling. Euryale hadn't been in Aphrodite's company since before the Gorgon's ouster, but hers was not a presence you would ever forget, regardless of how many years had gone by.

Aphrodite regarded them, and Asher sucked in a breath. Even though the logical part of her understood it was a normal reaction—any man would be dumbstruck in Aphrodite's presence—needles of jealousy pricked her. She had a brief, searing thought of slapping the arrogant goddess's leer off her face. Aphrodite was the goddess of love and beauty, and even in her earlier, more powerful goddess days, Euryale was nothing but a minor figure. If the woman dared to think she could take Asher from Euryale, she would…

What would you do, Gorgon?

He's mine.

A low tinkling laugh met her declaration. *Dear Gorgon, all men are mine if I want them.*

Her hands curled into fists as they approached the table. Euryale considered ways she could mess Aphrodite up. She could push her off her chair so that coifed hair would fall out of its intricate braid. She could throw dirt on her white outfit. She could…

"Sit down, both of you," Aphrodite said and raised her eyebrows at Harmonia, who took up a position behind the other woman, acting as Aphrodite's bodyguard.

Perhaps she was. After all, she was in the presence of a Gorgon who could be volatile. The notion caused a wicked grin to curve over Euryale's face.

A waiter scurried over and they ordered drinks. Harmonia stayed motionless, but Euryale, her lip curled minutely. Whether it was their quest or Asher's company that offended her, there was no question she did not care for them and did not want to be there. Some goddess of harmony and concord she was.

The attention of the café was riveted on the goddess. Men glanced toward Aphrodite and more than one tried to catch her eye. She bore it all with amusement, and a hint of predatory awareness, the sense that the interest was necessary for her survival.

The waiter hurried back bearing a tray that held more than drinks. He unloaded cubes of feta over fresh tomatoes and slices of bread with herbs sprinkled over the top. He also brought another plate of sliced tomatoes with cucumbers over them. He set it all down and bowed low, a slavish grin on his face.

Asher took a sip of the sparkling water and then raised an eyebrow at Aphrodite. Her return stare was amused and indulgent.

"I have one…two…" She examined the patrons in the café and several men tilted their glasses toward her. "All of the men in here are my admirers," She caught the eye of a woman sitting in the corner, "and the women, too," she said, and her voice was bright with mischief. "One of them brought us viands. How kind. Partake, please. These vegetables were picked this morning. You will not eat better for days."

As a monster, Euryale lived by the mantra of eating when food was available and sleeping when it was safe to do so. She reached for the feta and tomatoes while Asher did the same. Aphrodite gestured to Harmonia, who prepared a plate for Aphrodite and slid it in front of the goddess. Asher's sister glared at the duo again, her attitude that of someone who had caught you wearing muddy shoes in the house.

"What brings you to my island?" Aphrodite asked after a few minutes of quiet eating. The feta and tomatoes were delicious. It would be a long time before she would tire of tasting food again, instead of gobbling it up for sustenance and need, rather than flavor.

"You're aware of our quest," Asher said, wiping his mouth before grinning at Aphrodite. Bastard. How dare he sniff around Aphrodite that way.

Asher slid his hand over her leg and squeezed. Euryale let out a breath, some of the tension fading.

Aphrodite inclined her head. "I am. All of Olympus is. We are aware of the evil in our midst and that it comes ever closer. Why are you here?"

"Hebe said you might be able to help us. Give us answers."

"Did she?" Aphrodite summoned the waiter, who brought over a plate of olives. She picked through them and selected one, then ate it before continuing. "Gorgon, there is not much I can tell you. I feel the presence south, on Crete. Whoever it is, has hidden their mind from us. It was by happenstance that I learned that much. Men tell you a great deal when they are your bedfellows, and the last man had an encounter with these creatures and was lucky to escape. This was in Turkey, where they last struck."

Euryale glanced at Asher. "We were not aware of the Turkish situation. Was someone killed?"

Aphrodite waved a hand. "A minor god. As was this man, who was with him at the time and got away. He said the oddest things. He said that there was this great noise that was like the wind in the desert, and that everything was blocked out. The sound grew until it was all he could hear. He tried to run but was rooted to the spot. Then his friend, oh, what was that god's name…"

"Izih," Harmonia supplied, her gaze again going to Euryale. There was a meanness there, a hard expression that said there was no love lost between the two women.

"Yes, Izih, god of wild animals. He fell to the ground and began screaming, but it could not be heard in the din. Then he was still. Akbugha, the man I mentioned, was able to run away in the turmoil. He said the noise was unlike anything he had ever experienced." She studied Asher for so long that Euryale cleared her throat, and Aphrodite allowed herself a private smile. "You are acquainted with the power of sound, are you not, son of Roisin?"

"Yes. Of course. I'm a banshee."

"Ah, yes. Akbugha ran, but he could feel Izih's emotions through their mental connection. It appears that Izih did not shield as he was dying, or he needed Azbugha to appreciate what he was going through. The vibration expanded until it was akin to a living thing and then…nothing."

Euryale said nothing for several moments. She could almost feel the events unfolding. First the sound, which started small and then grew until the gods perceived it. Then they understood something was wrong. But they were gods, and what could harm them? Then the awareness that, no—this was something bad, and that momentary shock where you try to figure out what to do. Then…

Somewhere behind them, a noise had started.

* * *

"Asher!" Euryale shouted and Asher reacted on instinct, hurling himself toward her as she rolled. Aphrodite remained where she was, but Harmonia fell into a fighting stance. The tourist in the café gaped at them. The Greeks didn't take notice of the commotion. This noise was at a higher pitch than humans could hear. It wasn't meant for them; it was for the gods.

The cliff face was nearby when Euryale came out of her roll. Aphrodite continued to sip her tea and plucked at the olives. If she was disturbed by the noise, she gave no evidence of it.

"Euryale? Is it a setup? Are the bastards here?"

Euryale's focus snapped to Harmonia. "Did you do this?"

Harmonia's attention was directed to where the din was coming from. "You would think that, monster. We are not responsible for this. You have brought this blight to the island. How dare you?"

Aphrodite rose, still having every appearance of being unconcerned. The clamor grew until it was a shriek, and Asher couldn't imagine how Aphrodite could stand it. Even he, a banshee, was having trouble.

Harmonia whirled around. The source of the sound came from the bottom of the cliff. Asher ran to Euryale's side. She was still in a defensive crouch, her perception focused on the sand below. Around them the day was warm and breezy, but the racket dominated everything.

Aphrodite patted her lips and gestured to her daughter. Harmonia made a strangled noise and then crumpled.

The noise continued to rise.

"I'll be right back," Euryale said, and without another word, plunged off the cliff.

Asher's attention was split between the heartbreaking image of his woman plunging to the bottom, and his collapsed half-sister. As he watched, Euryale landed, and then was once again on her feet. It was then that he remembered one of her Gorgon talents was the ability to leap. He always believed that meant up and not down, but now he stood corrected.

Aphrodite summoned a waiter, and they pushed Harmonia onto a makeshift couch strung together with two chairs. The other patrons in the restaurant had given up any pretense of their conversations and watched the trio with avid interest. He had no time to wonder what they were thinking of Euryale's nosedive to the bottom of the cliff. He would worry about that in a moment. First, he turned to Aphrodite. She was patting her daughter's face with a wet cloth, her face still serene. No frown lines or imperfections marked her beautiful visage, but he detected a momentary flicker of concern.

"I have to get down to Euryale," he said, and Aphrodite glanced up. Now, pain flew across her face before it was gone, shuttered by a sanguine gaze that had to be a façade.

"Your Gorgon does not expect you to follow," the goddess replied. "She is far more experienced in this than you are."

"Nevertheless, I have to go down to her. Is Harmonia…will she be…what happened?"

"It is unclear. I believe your adversaries are taunting you."

He coughed, anger starting to flare within him. "They're your adversaries, too."

"This task was given to you, banshee. Do you not understand? This is your mission to complete. Our lives are at risk and so is yours if you do not do what is needed. These gods who think they can murder us must be stopped, and you must do it."

He paused. "Gods?"

She waved a hand toward the cliff face. "Only a god can kill a god. Why else would Athena bring a goddess into this? Did you ever wonder why your talents were needed? These criminals have the same skill set as you do, and therefore you are suited to combat them. Your Gorgon is down there wanting to take action, but she will not find your opponents. This is a mere way-stop. A pause in the proceedings, if you will."

He scanned the prone Harmonia. As he studied his half-sister, the sound cut off.

Aphrodite rose, barely glancing at her handmaiden. Asher would have been appalled at the lack of empathy before this quest, but she was a goddess. Compassion was not part of the package.

"There. It has ceased. You must move to your next destination and end this. Or everything you have struggled for will be for nothing."

"Next destination…" There was something else detectable in Asher's blasted ears, a trickle of sound that rose to a torrent.

"…come…come…we are waiting…"

* * *

She should have expected that the beach would be empty of deities.

The patrons sunning themselves on the strip of sand gave her an odd stare when she landed. Some looked up to the cliff top and then at her, appearing to wonder how it was possible for her to make such a dive. She didn't care. They wouldn't be here long enough for any meaningful questions.

Her gaze swept first from side to side and then she went up the rock, searching for any signs of life but could detect nothing except crags and tufts of grass. Their antagonists could be lurking in the rock face, waiting for their chance.

Asher's face appeared and then disappeared. She prowled the beach, searching for any clues. Euryale understood it was a trap. There was a reason why their enemy had not done more than scare them up until that point. Something was going to happen—on Crete. Crete was where the real battle would take place.

"Hey, how did you do that?"

A tanned blonde female surfer was gaping at her, mouth open, tongue visible.

"Do what?" She dusted off her shirt, doing her best to appear innocent.

"The cliff…" she said and raised a hand to point upward. "You…jumped?"

She shook her head. "Illusion. I was just a little way up. Right there." She pointed to a promising crag that she could suggest would be where she had been, rather than where she was. She didn't have the luxury of time to deal with the humans in this area. Most were turning back to their towels, uninterested in her.

The surfer continued to study her, a disbelieving expression on her face, until Euryale wondered if she was going to have to push her with her mind. She had been lured into doing something unwise, and now this kid was slowing her down.

Then the other woman backed up a step. "Sure, lady, whatever you say. Maybe I shouldn't have smoked that weed last night."

Euryale breathed out a sigh of relief.

"Maybe not," she agreed. "The sun will do odd things. You might need to take a break from surfing."

Then the surfer smirked, and Euryale detected the menace behind her appearance. Her weed-smoking surfer aspect had covered her true nature, but now Euryale understood it was an act.

"Did you like my war cry? There is more where that came from, Gorgon. Leave at once. Your destiny awaits on Crete. Do not tarry. Mother wishes to meet you."

The woman opened her mouth, and there was that piercing shriek again. Up close, it threatened to burst Euryale's eardrums, and she clapped her hands over her ears, watching the surfer girl screech. The woman shut her mouth, smirked at Euryale, and ran back along the sand. Once again, the humans showed no sign of hearing the noise. She hesitated a fraction of a second too long and the girl disappeared behind a rock.

She peered in all directions but found nothing. She searched on the mental plane and could detect nothing. There might have been a figure in the ocean, but there were many such shapes, and any one of them could have been the woman.

She focused again on the cliff face and then back to the sand. Then she returned her gaze to the ocean, puzzling out the girl's words. Her war cry. Her *war cry.*

Euryale knew who, and what, they were facing.

Chapter Fifteen

"Eris?" Asher asked, shaking his head. "You mentioned her before, and her children. You think this is the goddess we've been fighting? What brought you to that conclusion?"

They had hired a private yacht and sailed to Crete rather than try to arrange for a plane. These gods had been a step ahead of them this entire time. If they were revealing themselves now, it was because they wanted Euryale and Asher to be aware.

"Eris is the goddess of strife," Euryale said with the air of explaining things to a child.

"Shit, I already know that, but why aren't we flying to Crete? It will take too long by boat."

"We are going to Crete. We're just not flying there."

Asher gestured to the villa they had rented for the night and then out to where the sun was beginning to set. "You've altered our plan. Why?"

She was tired and heartsore. She couldn't recall ever being this weary. Understanding what they were facing made Euryale want to lie down and never get up. She desired to return to simpler times when monsters looked like monsters.

"Because it's what they expect. They showed their hand and expected us to go chasing after them. It was wise to stop and regroup. Plus, you had no comprehension of Eris and her helpers, and I didn't think you should go into battle unprepared."

Annoyance crossed Asher's face. She lay on the large bed, digging her hands into the coverlet. It was all so tiring. All she needed to do was sleep.

"Then tell me, oh, wise Gorgon. Why do you think they did this now, when they've remained hidden all these years? Why show themselves to you, to us?"

His words cut into her soul. Despite herself, she had gotten tangled up with Asher. It was more than just the physical, it had gone into the emotional and spiritual as well. She didn't know how to tell him that, if this was going to be their final moments together, she would delay their arrival as long as she could. She either needed to tell him or try and keep lying.

"You're right, Asher, it isn't why I opted for the yacht," she said with a tone so weary, that he paused in whatever it was he'd been about to say, and studied her.

He spread his hands, his forehead creasing. "I don't understand," he said and sat down next to her. The bedsprings creaked as they accepted his weight.

Euryale rolled over and slid her hand into his.

"We might not survive this. I needed to spend a little more time with you before we faced the danger of this situation."

He breathed out and then squeezed her fingers. "I was hoping that was the reason. I want to steal more moments with you as well."

His hair was getting longer. Soon it would be more like that of the Greek gods of old, with curling locks framing his face. If he grew a beard, he could complete the image.

"You don't mind?"

"That you want to be with me? Of course not. I've got something to show you," he said with a wicked grin. "But first, tell me about Eris, and what we're walking into."

* * *

Her voice washed over him as Euryale relayed what she could tell him about their adversaries. He closed his eyes, letting the mental images play out.

"Eris is the Greek goddess of strife and discord. She is also the one who initiated the Trojan War by causing the Judgment of Paris. Her Apple of Discord made the Greek goddesses quarrel. She had been snubbed by a lack of an invitation to a wedding—I forget which one—and went there for the express purpose of causing trouble."

Asher was aware Euryale was giving him important information, but all he sought right then was to be with Euryale. He let the words continue to sweep over him until a response was required. "Not being invited to a wedding sounds fine to me. Go on."

She stroked his forehead with a gentle touch and turned his face into her hand.

"She tossed the apple into the proceedings where Paris was supposed to choose the fairest goddess of all. Each of the vain witches tried to bribe him, and he chose Aphrodite, which caused no end of trouble."

"I haven't met Athena, but from what you've said, I'd pick Aphrodite as well," he said without stirring. Her touch was like a balm to his senses, making his body stir.

"Don't let Athena hear you say that," Euryale warned. "It led to the Trojan War. But that was by far the least of Eris's mischief. She is the goddess of strife, that is what she does. But that's not her view, of course. She believed that without chaos, life would be boring."

"What about the rest? She's not working alone. We've encountered more than one person."

Euryale shifted, and Asher turned until he was half laying on her. She put her arms around him and held him. He reveled in the warmth of her body. This might be the last night they had together. He burrowed down, pressing a kiss against her side as he stretched out.

"That's right. She has a religion, from what I understand, but this is more basic. I believe we are dealing with the Machai. They are the spirits, or daemons of battle and combat. They are her sons and daughters, and loyal to her. The being I came across today had to be Alala, who is the personification of war-cry."

He chuckled. "Must suck to have such a specific job."

Her fingers stilled. "Is that so different than a banshee? You ululate when a person is dying, so the legends go. That's pretty exact."

He groaned. "Point taken. We do more than shriek when people are dying."

"Yet, that is your legend."

"Yes," he agreed, grateful when she started stroking his head again. He could stay curled up with her forever.

"It explains why we haven't had any sign of their presence until they revealed themselves. They stick together, so none of them would talk."

"Alala wanted you to recognize who they were," he mused. "Why?"

Euryale's mouth twisted to the side, and she made an unhappy gesture with her shoulders. "Many reasons are possible. I couldn't say which one is the truth. They might be tired of running. It's probable they have a trap they are going to spring. Perhaps this is what they do when they are focused on an enemy. There is no way to know for sure until it happens."

"And the museum? Who were those creatures causing that?"

"Likely that was Homados, who is battle-noise, and Kydoimos, who is confusion. The beasts were likely commanded to do their bidding, or they were cyphers. They have been sprinkling clues for us the entire time, and we were too witless to figure it out. They threw Alala in our path to seal the understanding."

"Is this like the part of the movie where the enemy reveals his plot before killing the hero?" Asher asked and kissed her neck. "Because that doesn't work out so well in movies."

She leaned down until her lips were just a breath apart from his. "This isn't the movies," she replied.

"No, it's not. Why is Eris doing this? You said she's the goddess of strife but that is about causing trouble, not killing gods."

Euryale ran her hands along his back and Asher groaned. Just one touch from her and he was on fire, craving nothing but the taste of her. She had been right to wait to leave until the morning. If this was to be their last night together, then he was going to take advantage and give her an evening that she would never forget.

"I can't speak to another goddess's motives," she said and kissed him again.

"Maybe she was bored. Eternity is a long time. She could want to shake up the pantheon and take her place as a major goddess. It is impossible to know the minds of gods."

"But you're a goddess."

"Hence my point," she said in a teasing tone that stirred his body to life again. The hairs on his forearm rose at her nearness. His skin was hot, like lava. He turned, rolling onto his back and yanking her to him. She went without hesitation, and his cock hardened. There was more to show her and more to experience. Maybe for the first and last time. But that was for tomorrow. Tonight was about the woman in his arms.

With that plan in mind, Asher bent to kiss Euryale in earnest.

* * *

His touch was streaks of wildfire setting her nerves aflame. When he caressed her, the heavens opened up. He ran gentle fingers across her belly, and it contracted. Euryale shivered, although the night was warm. The breeze lifted the gauzy curtains, and she could hear the crash of the waves around them.

He kissed her, his embrace gentle and then more fervent. With her head cupped in his hands he delved his tongue inside her mouth, and the heat and warmth of him was like a fire in her soul. She loved this man. It was as simple and as profound as that.

He stroked her skin, trailing his fingers down her collarbone and body. Euryale tugged at his shirt and he lifted his arms, letting her pull it over his head. She marveled at the expanse of his chest, the carved muscles, and dusting of hair.

"I want to see you, too," he whispered and moved so that he could pull her shirt off.

"I want to see all of you," he said, "Ah, Euryale, you're so beautiful."

It wasn't something she was used to hearing, but the blatant admiration in his gaze as he swept it over her peaks left no doubt that he meant every word.

They divested themselves of their remaining clothing and returned to the bed. Euryale was thrilled to find his hard penis ready for her, its magnificent length a wonder all its own.

He bent to his ministrations, moving his lips down her body in gentle kisses, following the trail of his hands. He kissed her shoulder, her collarbone and then down, planting kisses on the side and top of her breasts until she arched out and clutched at his hair. Euryale began panting in gasps as excitement grew inside her.

Then he claimed one hard nipple and Euryale shrieked from the bliss of it. Shock waves rippled through her at the warm, wet feeling of his tongue and mouth. Her body erupted in goose bumps and pleasure, and she came close to climaxing right then.

He alternated between breasts, treating each high peak with equal attention, until Euryale no longer had control of herself. She was slick with moisture, and her hips thrust against him, wanting, needing to feel his hardness so she could be complete.

"I want to be inside you," he whispered and nipped on her earlobe.

"Good. Because that's where I want you to be," she replied, nipping his ear in return before running her tongue down his jawline, then to his neck. He took his cock in his hand and opened her to him with his organ.

Meeting her gaze, he slid the tip of him inside and filled her inch by inch, his erect penis pushing its way inside. When he was fully sheathed, he leaned forward, bracing himself on his forearms.

"Oh, god," she said, already near climax. He began stroking her, pulling out and then plunging back in. She clutched at him, throwing her head back and digging her hands into his shoulders.

She put her ankles around his waist and drew him in as deep as she could. "Oh, god," she said again. "I…" She broke off, streams of ecstasy flooding her. She arched against him, her hips moving under his.

His eyes were dark with pleasure when she met them again. Then he closed them and began thrusting hard, the muscles in his butt clenching. He dropped to her body and hauled her against him, his movements wild. He moaned against her ear and warmth flooded her as his body rippled. He cried out, gathering her to him for one final push as he bared his teeth, their bodies so close it was like they were one person.

They both came back to earth, her head resting on the pillow, his on her neck.

Her heart was so full it was all she could do not to tell him how she felt. But this was not the time nor the place to do so.

* * *

The yacht was swift, and they were making good time toward their next, and final destination. The captain was a taciturn man, saying little, which suited Asher just fine.

"You're the one who understands these people," Asher said as they hovered over a tablet in the salon, uncaring of the gorgeous Aegean Sea flowing around them. Under different circumstances, he would be out on deck enjoying the sight of the amazing view. There was no time for that. He had to protect his woman and, to do that, he had to stop a goddess and her children. Asher hid from Euryale how unequal he was to the task. He felt as though he was more banshee than god, with little interest in the affairs of the pantheons. Now he was thrust in the middle of an age-old war, and he wouldn't care, *if* the fate of the woman he loved didn't hang in the balance. He had no doubt that if they failed, Euryale would once again be turned into a monster and be killed. He couldn't bear to witness the humanity flee from her face and be replaced by the rapier glare of a fiend. If his life was the only one to be sacrificed if they failed, he wouldn't have minded so much, but his mother's life also hung in the balance. Two women he loved were counting on him not to fail.

"I had little interaction with Eris, but I am more familiar with her than you are. She was a strange sort of goddess, more interested in stirring up trouble than anything else. But I suppose that was her nature, just as it is Aphrodite's to be adored."

He studied Euryale for a moment, memorizing the fall of her hair and the curve of her chin. He yearned to tell her of his love but had to wait.

"What's the plan?"

She glanced at the water and back to him. "They're expecting us. This entire journey has been one long setup to get us to Crete. It has to be a trap. Otherwise they would have attacked us instead of sending their forays, like the first strike in Los Angeles. They may be ready to reveal themselves to the gods and are using our quest to do so."

"Shouldn't we tell Athena and Ares? We found out who the culprits are—can't they step in now?"

Euryale let out a bitter laugh. "Gods don't do their own dirty work unless something is in it for them. They gave this task to us to complete. They may already realize it's Eris and opted to let us find the clues and follow the leads instead of telling us. They are nobody's friend."

Shit.

Now was not the time to remind her again that she was an immortal goddess, but Asher was silent for so long that the knowledge crossed her face. Euryale's expression shifted to distaste and then a wry sort of humor.

The boat continued to glide toward their destination, the motor audible over the waves. The sea was choppy, but the skies were clear and there was no hint of a storm. It was a perfect Aegean day, and everything would have been idyllic, if not for the fact that they were heading toward a confrontation with god killers, with their lives on the line.

"Would you resurrect if they murdered you?"

Her mouth twisted into a parody of a smile before it fell into a downward curve.

"It's impossible to know. We have been monsters for so long, that I am not sure what goddess powers we retained."

"I can't lose you."

It was as close as he could get to saying what he really meant. He waited, but she said nothing in reply.

"We're almost to the island," the captain said, and they both turned to face the image of Crete looming on the horizon. Asher had wanted to visit the Greek islands for decades but never had the chance. Now he wished he was anywhere else. Here was where their enemies awaited, and with it, an uncertain outcome that promised only disaster.

The foremost tragedy would be losing Euryale. His life meant nothing against that.

Chapter Sixteen

Euryale didn't remember the Minoans; their time predated her existence. The remnants of their bull cult were everywhere in the ruins, especially in the minotaur, who was a creature even more beleaguered than her. Crete was a gorgeous island, rocky and craggy like all the Greek islands, with the shattered evidence of the former Minoan culture throughout the landscape.

Like all Greek islands, it was not as built-up as the cities, but it was denser than many. Given its size, it was no surprise it had housed many great civilizations pre and post the Minoans. By the time the Romans ruled, post-Minoans, she was already a monster and traveling to islands was both difficult and unwise. Euryale eschewed islands, even larger ones like this one, in favor of wild mainland areas where caves and forests made for good hiding places.

Now that she was back in her original form, she would explore sites like this that had been off limits to her. While she had been a monster, she cared little about the rest of the world. Now she understood how much there was to it, and how much she had missed all these centuries. There was so much to go to now, that she didn't need to limit her time and energy. She and Asher would discover the world when this was done, and not just the hidden places.

That was, if they survived.

"Can you feel them? Do you know where to look?" Asher's voice was low and urgent.

"I haven't a clue."

The landscape was sun-drenched as most Greek islands were, the intense rays reflecting off the rocks and the white buildings until it was almost blinding.

"I think I do. We use our voices. That's what we both have in common. That isn't a coincidence. You can leap, and I have superior strength like my father. There's a reason the gods put us together."

She turned on him, fury gathering. She lashed out before she could stop herself. "Did it ever occur to you that the gods sent us on this quest because we were expendable? So that they wouldn't have to risk their own hides? Nothing can get to them in Olympus. They are safe there. Eris and her minions can't touch them there. They can leave, sure, but why do they care? They can send people like us to do their dirty work. For all we know, we aren't the first to try and stop these people, and if we fail, they will dispatch others. Don't be so smug about the gods 'putting us together.' They did it to save themselves. If we lose, *they* lose nothing."

He put his hands on her hips and urged her to him. She had a momentary idea of resisting but decided otherwise. The feel of him was smooth and warm and so right.

"Fuck, Euryale, I'm scared, too," he murmured against her ear before he drew her into a hard embrace.

His hands trembled, evidence he was telling the truth. She took in a deep breath and met his eyes. They had been together through all of this, and now they would be strong one last time.

"How did you figure that out?" she asked. There were shadows on his face, a bruised quality under his eyes. It made her love him more than she believed possible.

That was more terrifying than the gods out for their destruction.

"You're picking a fight. That's what you do when you're scared. You're not driving me off that way, Euryale. You and me, we're going to stay and fight—and win."

She tried to be mad and it was impossible. Despite the situation, she grinned.

"You are getting to understand me well. You are right. I'm scared. But I also want this over with. We have a job to do, so let's go do it."

"First a kiss," he demanded and claimed her lips. He smelled of the sea and of man, the earthy rich scent of him filling her nostrils. She pressed against him, allowing herself one more instant to feel his strong body, the hard planes of him, and the essential maleness that made him her beloved Asher. She could wish for so many things to be different, but she would change nothing about this moment.

Moments, like all things, passed, and they separated. She almost whimpered with regret but said nothing as she stepped back and took his now-outstretched hand.

"You're right. We use our combined powers to fight. I need to call my sister."

Euryale retreated to where Asher was out of earshot. She dialed her sibling. While she waited, hoping that the call would go through, she rehearsed what she would say.

"Euryale," Stheno said when she answered. The line was hissing, filled with static and the buzz of other voices in the distance. "Where are you?"

"Crete. Our final battle is upon us."

Stheno sucked in a breath. "Why did you not tell me sooner? Do you need me there? If so, I will arrange to get there within the day."

Euryale shook her head, forgetting Stheno could not observe her. "No, Sister. This is our task. I will do my duty and fulfill it. Besides, I have another mission for you."

Stheno's silence was profound, saying all the things that needed to be said, only without words. The sisters had been each other's only source of strength and comfort for too long for Euryale not to be aware of what her sister was feeling.

"I am already arranging to go to Medusa's cave. It is not so easy to do in this day and age," she replied. "But that is not the task, is it?"

Euryale debated the many ways to answer that question. After all these years, there could be no falsehood, no dissembling between the two sisters.

"It isn't. I love you very much, Stheno, and you are the only one I can trust with this. Stheno, if I fail, or if Athena plays me false then…you must avenge me. It is why you cannot come here. I need you to be away from this. Asher and I will do what needs to be done. Promise me you will punish the goddess if she lies. Will you do that for me?"

Stheno let out a ragged, harsh breath. "Oh, Sister, of course I will. Only I would do it whether Athena plays you false or not. That bitch has gotten away with too much for too long."

"No," Euryale said, shaking her head, forgetting again Stheno only had audio capabilities at the moment. "Only if she is deceitful. Promise me, Stheno. By the love you bear for me, promise."

For several seconds Euryale thought Stheno wasn't going to agree. "I would rather be there, Sister, but I will grant you this. I do understand about oaths and battles. I love you, too, sister mine, and I swear that Athena will not go unpunished if she betrays you."

Euryale debated how to ask the next thing before deciding just to ask.

"May I ask it of my companion as well?"

Stheno let out something close to a growl. "This is between sisters only."

"Promise me you will consider it. Thank you, Stheno. You are the only one I can trust."

"Always."

* * *

He had expected the violence to start the moment they landed, as it had on Kythira, but to his surprise, there was no sign of their adversaries. He was tensed for it, almost wished for it, but nothing occurred. They joined a tour of the Minoan ruins. No attack happened. They went down to the water, where the terrible tsunami that resulted from the explosion at Thera three thousand years ago, had swept onto the shore and devastated the Minoans, and waited. Nothing.

As the hours dragged on, Asher became more and more tense. He wished for it to begin, damn it, so that they could do what they'd been sent to do.

The others were better prepared and had superior weaponry. This was an unequal match. Nonetheless, he'd promised, and for the woman he loved, he would fight to his dying breath. It was all he could do. To protect Euryale, his impossible Gorgon, he was willing to die. That should satisfy the bloodthirsty

Ares, if it came to that.

They first went to Vai Beach, which was backed by Europe's largest natural date palm forest. The longer he waited for the attack to happen, the more uneasy he became.

"Why don't they strike?" Asher peered out over the waves, detecting nothing but ocean and the spires of rocks in the water. The water was a startling blue that was a signature of the Mediterranean waters, but today he took no pleasure in its beauty.

"They are toying with us," Euryale said.

"Do we find them, or do they find us?" He gestured behind them. "I guess there's a monastery nearby and another set of ruins close at hand. Is that where we're supposed to go? We've been trailing them all this time and now that we're here, I have no idea what happens next."

"Neither do I, Asher. I suggested Vai Beach just to give us a starting point. Rousolakkos, the Minoan city you mentioned, is a possibility for the showdown, but only that. Eris is unpredictable, as she has proven throughout this adventure. I can't tell what she is going to do next, or what we are to do." Her face shifted, her eyebrows drawing together and her mouth tightening. For a moment, she seemed decades older than her mid-twenties appearance. "I had one job for all these millennia—survive. Sometimes I think it would be easier if I were still a monster."

Asher's breath stopped. "Don't say that. It's not true. You deserve to be a woman."

"Maybe." She said it with slow words, as though with an effort. He couldn't penetrate her mind, but her body was drooping, her hands dragging toward the sand as though with sorrow. He moved toward her to gather her close.

Before he could, a woman ran up to them. Asher flinched and moved to step in front of Euryale, but she pushed him aside and stood next to him.

"Have you been to the pink beach?" She had an American accent and Asher's forehead creased in puzzlement.

"The…what?"

The perky female waved a hand in an uncertain direction. "The pink beach. Elafonissi or something. I hear it's amazing. You should check it out."

"Um, okay." Asher gave Euryale a puzzled glance. She was studying the person with a flicker of unease beyond her stoic appearance.

Euryale?

She has shields that are too powerful for a human. There is something strange here.

The person pointed toward the distance and Asher's attention swung that way. Out of the corner of his eye, he detected another person hovering nearby, but they were gone when he focused on the woman again.

"It's that way. The other side of the island. It's about five hours from here, but it is well worth the trip. You need to go. By nightfall."

Euryale tilted her head and the being shifted her gaze away. Euryale frowned, her attention going to the woman's face again.

"I understand now. Tell your…friends…that we received their message. Aite." She said the word not as a form of eaten but as a proper name. The woman held out her hands like a priest giving a benediction. But there was no salvation here.

"Good. I'm glad you're not as stupid as we thought. They will be waiting. It is time."

The person ran off, joining a crowd of friends who stood a little way off. Asher and Euryale stared after her.

"She was something other than human," Asher said.

"Yes."

"Who or what is Aite?"

She followed the route of the woman who had disappeared around the bend. The waves continued to lap, bringing in foam and the brilliant blue water, but Asher couldn't take any pleasure in it. After all this time and all this chasing, the hour was upon them.

"Aite is another descendant of Eris. She's the goddess of mischief and folly, and other things such as ruin. She's a messenger, nothing more. Now we have our next destination: Elafonissi beach. We will have to discover what awaits us there in the morning."

No. Do not wait until morning. That will be too late.

The unfamiliar mental voice boomed through his shields, making him wince. "Aite said we had to get there by nightfall. I think we need to."

Euryale met his eyes with a blank stare and then shuddered.

"You're right, she did. That is what we must do."

* * *

They arrived at the location as the sun was setting. Their rented car was parked in a dirt and gravel parking lot off to the side that was emptying of cars with every passing moment. Elafonissi Beach or Lagoon was on the southwestern side of Crete and was technically a different island. It was within walking distance from the mainland along a sand spar that rose up high enough that people did not have to worry about water as they walked across. People were packing in for the night, and they were going against traffic as they went to their destination. The island itself was protected, and on many lists for being one of the most beautiful beaches in the world.

Euryale had no doubt that it was, but the pink-hued sand was lost on her. What were Eris and her Machai thinking to take the fight to a place like this? The Chrysoskalitisa monastery lay five kilometers away. Everything about this place screamed somewhere sacred that should not be fouled with the fights of gods. But that was a goddess for you—uncaring of the affairs of man or the land he inhabited.

"You are missing the good stuff," a man said. He had a beach umbrella and his family lingered behind him as they trudged to the car. "It's the color you come for, which you aren't going to be able to appreciate in the dark."

This time, Euryale received nothing but well-meaning hospitality from the man and nodded to him.

"We got here too late, but we hear it isn't to be missed. We came right away."

"Yeah, I get that. There's way more to enjoy when the sun is up. You should go now. It's not safe."

It was in several people's minds that they would have stayed for the sunset, but instead they were compelled to leave the island. It appeared that Eris did not want an audience for this showdown. That suited Euryale fine. The more innocent bystanders out of the way the better.

"We'll come back in the morning, too," Asher said. He took Euryale's hand, and they walked toward the spar of sand that connected Crete from the island.

At low tide, as it was now, they could walk across without getting their feet wet. She wondered if that was something else that Eris had planned. It had always been intended that they would come to this beach, at a time and place of Eris's choosing to do this. The rest had just been window dressing.

Euryale gripped Asher's arm, forcing him to stop. Dread flooded her, a suspicion rising in her consciousness like the waves lapping at the shore.

"Asher…if we aren't the fighters, but the sacrifices, let's go down swinging."

"We're not going to die."

The sun was beginning to set around them, lighting up the sky in brilliant hues. It was glorious, and at another time, she might have enjoyed the beauty of the moment.

"Asher, if they turned me back to a woman and sent you to me not because we have so-called compatible powers but because we are disposable, we need to fight with all that we have. Well, maybe I'm the one who's expendable."

"Expendable…" He blinked; the word thick on his tongue. "You think my father was ready to forfeit me to save his ass? That he used my promise to throw me into the fire?"

He was so bereft, so unable to comprehend what he was saying, that she went to him. It was as natural as breathing, as perfect as the gorgeous beach, to put her arms around him and hold him close. Asher's body pressed against hers, and he buried his face in her hair.

"I think it's possible. I rule out nothing when it comes to the gods."

"It didn't cross my mind, Euryale. All this time I've been thinking we were the ones for this job and only we could do it, for whatever reason. But what you're saying makes a lot more sense. You and I were both in debt to the gods and we had to go on this mission. If we're hurt or killed, they're still safe." He moved his head and grazed a kiss over her ear, her cheek and then her lips. She sighed, never wanting the moment to end.

The way to move forward was to face this head-on. They may have been forced into this position, but she would stay true to her oath. She had not only herself, but her sisters to think of. No matter what, Euryale had made a promise and she would honor that.

"They will answer to us when this is through," Asher said and cupped her face. Euryale nearly cried at the touch of a half banshee who had shown her more of what it meant to be loved than anyone in her entire life. Even her sisters, who loved her beyond reason, had never made her feel like this. He would forever be the one man who could get to her.

And after this, she would lose him. There was nothing to be done. She kissed him, feathering her hand through his thick hair.

"They are gods. Many people have tried to get them to answer for their arrogance, but it never works. They do not care about others. Come, let's find out what hand the fates and the gods have dealt us."

He took her hand and they focused on the island in the diminishing light. There was stillness all around them, an unnatural quiet. Even the waves rippled low, their power muted. That was impossible, though. Eris was a goddess of mayhem. Neither she nor her minions had any power over water.

Yet just as she thought it, Euryale caught a glimpse of something. Visible just out of the corner of her eye, something moved.

Chapter Seventeen

A flock of sandpipers erupted from behind a nearby rock. The birds made distressed noises as they traveled upward before heading toward the mainland of Crete.

No sooner had they started to fade than fish began flopping onto the sand and then back down into the water, their bodies making slapping sounds. The waves crashed against his ears like sonic booms. Asher's heart pounded frantically as he tried to find the source of the frenzy. Seagulls flowed in, trying to pick off the fish, their caws loud, adding to the cacophony around them. Another covey of birds was flushed from somewhere, but all Asher could hear was the beating of their wings as they also took to the sky. For one crazed moment, he assumed the birds were going to attack them ala the old Hitchcock movie, but they dashed off. Then the seagulls took off as well, abandoning the fish, and their protesting caws trailed behind them as they left.

"*Kydoimos*," Euryale shouted, ducking to avoid the gulls as they winged into the air. Some got so close, he could have reached out and batted them down.

"What?" He had to shout over the fleeing birds.

"Kydoimos," she repeated. "Machai of confusion. She is one of Eris's helpers. We've encountered her before."

"No question, we're in the right place then."

"None at all," she agreed and pointed to a rock not too far away. "Come on. Let's get to shelter."

They ran for the rock, and had just gotten there, when a herd of goats charged toward them, rushing to where they had been standing and then stampeding toward them. At the last moment, they turned off and stampeded past, bleating as they went.

"Proioxis," Euryale said. "Onrush. They are trying to unnerve us."

He swallowed. "They're doing a good job."

A pack of barking dogs now assailed them, but once again, veered off before they reached the duo. These were meant to demoralize, not attack.

"What's next?" he asked, exasperated. He tested his banshee voice and found it ready.

The dogs came back the other way, barking louder this time, heading through them, and back the way they came.

"Palioxis," Euryale said. "Backrush."

"How many more are there?"

"Two more Machai. I fear there are more daemons that Eris has persuaded to join her cause. You don't want me to tell you how many."

"No, I probably don't."

Without warning a din split the air, loud and fierce, a whoop that pierced the molecules around them. There were voices in that cry, a thousand soldiers marching toward battle and shouting at the same time. It filled the space as a tangible thing. Asher rose, stepping forward and ignoring the few remaining dogs that lingered after the rest of the pack had gone. A goat opened its mouth, but Asher could hear no sound over the hubbub.

We've heard this one before.

No. This is Homados. Daemon of Battle Noise. You're thinking of Alala, daemon of War-Cry. Yes. We did hear this one before, at the museum.

Whoever it is, they're annoying.

Without warning, the clamor fell away. The animals made no further move toward them. Whatever had compelled the packs had stopped, and the creatures were going back to their normal behavior. His banshee self pushed at him, wanting to answer the war cry with his own blare, and show them what a *true* wailing creature sounded like. He peeked at Euryale, waiting for some cue of what to do. She was more experienced in these areas than he was. She was going to be far better in battle than him, that much he knew, despite his superior size. She was older, with more relevant talents. However, he was *not* without weapons, and he would use every one of them to protect her.

A hush settled over the island, the calm before the storm. Even the waves were quieter, their foam timid against the sand. The dogs and goats that were left behind wheeled off, darting on the sandbar back to the main island of Crete. He glanced up into the fading sky, but the birds were gone. They were alone.

"How will Eris explain this?" he asked, waving toward the empty place. "She scared off all the tourists. They will talk."

"I doubt anyone will even remember to comment on it. They won't be here, but they will have no recollection of why they left. That will be enough."

He shook his head. "You gods are something. I'm glad I'm only half god."

"There are advantages to being divine," she said and there was a sort of bleak humor in her reply.

Another horrible wail started again, and this time, Asher did recognize it. He didn't need Euryale to tell him that this was Alala, daemon of war-cry. The familiar, shrill sound shivered in his bones and turned them to water. It went through him like a lance, robbing him of spirit, of volition, and of courage. All he could think about was to turn and run…and that would be giving Alala what she wanted.

When they stayed where they were, the sound faded away and then stopped. Now the real battle would begin. He shuddered and shook himself to rid his body of the lingering trauma and doubt.

Euryale moved forward onto the spit of sand and raised her hands to the sky. She threw her head back and howled. The sound cut off.

"That…is…enough," she cried and flung her arms away from her body.

* * *

Who the hell did these daemons think they were? They were playing with a goddess and a demigod. They were less than nothing, and she would take care of them.

Euryale's sonic power rumbled in her vocal cords.

There was an eerie glow that moved across the water and surrounded the area, bathing them in its otherworldly light. The pink sand under their feet was now tinted green by the illumination. Asher stood poised next to her in a stance of readiness, taking in their surroundings.

As though descending from Olympus, Eris floated toward them. While it had been centuries since Euryale had beheld the goddess of discord, there was no mistaking her.

She was about Euryale's height, and slender. Her black hair was plaited in intricate braids with a few strands loose, a hairstyle unsuited for the battlefield. Her armor was carved with elaborate designs, a neckpiece that appeared to have pearls on it protecting that part of her body. The entire ensemble was bathed in that odd yellowish-green light, lending her eyes a haunted glow.

Eris landed on the sand, her hand outstretched. Asher stared at the object in her palm. Euryale laughed, ignoring the thing Eris was holding.

"Really, Eris? The apple of discord? Do you think it would be so easy to stir up trouble with me and Asher by tossing that apple into our midst? We are not vain goddesses to let that sorry piece of fruit have any effect. I was a monster for too long for my aspect to have any bearing on my actions."

Eris, who had the same perfect appearance as any goddess, with high cheekbones and smooth, aquiline features, tossed it aside.

"You know how it is with gods, Euryale, or perhaps you have forgotten. We do what is expected."

Asher tensed and Euryale wondered if he was going to attack the woman.

Be cautious, Asher. She is baiting us.

I can take her.

Not yet.

"There is truth in that," Euryale said.

"Why are you killing gods?" Asher demanded, moving toward Eris with an aggressive walk. Euryale sent him a warning and he stopped.

"That is not your concern, son of Ares," Eris said, examining her fingertips before casting an amused glance at Euryale. At one time, it would not have been unrealistic to think they could have been allies.

"You are wrong," Asher retorted. "My mother made a promise when I was born, and now, I *am* fulfilling that bargain. Our lives are lost if I don't. I don't care so much for myself, but I *do* care about my mother—*and* Euryale. Therefore, it *is* my issue."

Eris raised an eyebrow. Her manner was so languid they might have been in her sitting room discussing the day.

"And you, Gorgon? You have no love for other deities. Why do you continue on this quest? You owe them nothing."

The gods were vain and cruel and had never shown Euryale anything but harshness. She had no reason to chase Eris. She wavered, her balance and her mind at once unsteady. Eris's eyes glittered, that strange green light flickering. A warning went off in Euryale's head and she glanced around. While she could detect no sign of others, they had to be around.

"I pledged an oath when Athena released me from my other form. I do not break my vows," Euryale said. She made her statement formal, a decree. She could not spot the Machai, but they had to be somewhere close by. There was no question the daemons were around, but she was unsure who else might be with them. Eris had many kin.

"Ah," Eris said and turned her hands up in an "oh, well" gesture. "That is a pity. It would have made this so much simpler if you were."

Another figure emerged from the direction where the dogs had been. "Horkos," Euryale called to the slim man clad in a toga. "We are not oath breakers. You have no jurisdiction here."

The god, Horkos, son of Eris, had a face twisted with rage. No wonder. There were more oath breakers in the world than there were pure folk. If Euryale or Asher had said anything other than that they would honor their vow, Horkos could have attacked them in righteous retribution.

Horkos glanced from his mother to the pair. He opened his mouth, but no sound came out. Euryale began to understand how Eris had achieved this end. She preyed on the vulnerabilities of each victim and assigned her vast descendants to the person, each to their weakness. Eris sighed and waved her hand at her child. He grimaced and retreated, glaring at them as he went, with the appearance of someone who was sure they had been oath breakers and he should just take them out. Eris glared at her son and he left. Euryale breathed a sigh of relief. Eris was still following the rules of their stations, which could be an advantage if Euryale could figure out how. Eris had her—them—outnumbered and outmaneuvered, but there had to be an angle, or Eris would have dispatched them by now.

She looked around at the beautiful beach, not observing their surroundings. Euryale could not determine if there were more of Eris's children around, but there had to be. Eris would not come alone to this battle. She had not come this far by being weak or sympathetic to others.

"Why?" Asher asked and there was a wealth of questions in that simple word. He moved so that he was between Euryale and Eris, a move which the other goddess noted. She raised one eyebrow and considered the other woman.

He is showing his feeble side.

Euryale said nothing, but Eris's words went through her like a cannon.

He is a good man.

There is no such thing where the sons of the Greek gods are concerned.

"Eris is angry about being shunned by the gods, isn't that right, goddess of strife?"

Eris's hands were as festooned with jewelry as her chest plate and neckline. The pearls, which showed at her throat, carried through to a bracelet at her wrist, as well as a ring. The bracelets crawled up her arm and almost each finger boasted a ring. Despite the riot of adornments, it all belonged there as though it was part of her. Eris had a timeless appearance, as suited her ancient goddess status. If not for what she was doing, and the threat she presented to her and Asher, Euryale might have felt compassionate toward the other one. Eris was not the only goddess to be disregarded and dismissed by the Greek gods.

To feel sympathy for Eris was to risk her monster side and Euryale could not do that. She had made a promise and Gorgons fulfilled their promises, even when the gods who demanded them were false.

Euryale tried to dip into Eris's mind, but she had less luck than the other goddess at breaching shields.

"My reasons are my own. I will give you one chance, Gorgon. You have been wronged as so many of us have. Walk away now. Abandon this son of Ares and go. I will let you depart this battle. You do not need to be concerned with this."

Asher shot Euryale a quick glance. "Take her up on it, Euryale. Go. I will handle it. You would be safe that way."

"No way, Asher."

He stepped in front of her, blocking her line of sight to Eris.

"No, Asher. Not a chance. If I leave, you die."

"I'll take that gamble."

Her breath caught. No man had ever done that for her.

"No, you will not."

Eris examined her fingernails. "This is beginning to bore me. I am counting the moments, Gorgon. Leave him and join me. I will do more for you than the sons and daughters of Cronus ever will."

"Do it, Euryale. Please."

"No."

Eris met her gaze.

You fool. You should have left.

Not without you.

Once again, she tried to penetrate Eris's shields and could not.

Eris turned away, showing them her back. Asher moved to attack her, but Euryale grabbed his arm.

"Never strike a man when his back is turned," she hissed. "It shows cowardice. Wait."

"Last chance to go," he said, pointing toward the faint outline of buildings in the distance.

"I am not leaving. Stop asking."

Eris faced them again, her body sagging as though disappointed.

"Ah, Euryale, it is a shame I will have to kill you. I gave you a good option and you turned me down. Now, both of you will pay the price."

She raised her hands, and everything went dark.

Chapter Eighteen

Aite coalesced from shadows and mist. Although Asher was aware it was an illusion, it was a damned good one.

"Is it time, Mother?" She joined Eris on her place on the sand. The other goddess made a motion, and the same light that had shone before appeared.

Asher gasped as the light exposed at least a dozen figures standing behind Aite, ready for battle. They were outnumbered. There was no way to win. There was no way to fight these things and succeed. It was hopeless. They were going to perish.

He didn't want to die, but he'd lived a hundred years, and while that was a drop in the bucket compared to most of the people in his life, it was a long time. Maybe long enough, if it came to that. It was Euryale he was concerned about. She was no longer a monster, and should have a chance to enjoy that freedom. To have Eris snatch it away from her just wasn't fair.

"It is time, daughter. Their hubris is the height of folly. Do as you will."

Aite growled and focused her attention on first Euryale and then Asher. "The man will be a nice snack. But it's the woman I want."

"Do not be too hard on Euryale," Eris said. "She lost a lot in her centuries as a monster."

"At least I knew what I was. What's your excuse?" Euryale snapped off the words in quick succession.

Eris flung out a hand to stop her daughter before she could advance on the pair. Aite paused, her body still straining forward. "You dare ask me that?"

"I do. Why do you maintain the persona that you were back when I was human? The Greek gods will never change, but they could. So could you. Why do you persist?"

"They owe me." She lowered her arm. "You may continue, Aite. Goodbye, Gorgon. You should have joined me."

"Prepare to die." Aite raised her arms. Like Eris, her chest plate was sculpted. There were claws at the end of her fingers, in what Asher assumed were gloves or gauntlets, but then he recognized those were her real hands. The person before had been glamoured. She growled.

Another joined her and Asher shot a quick glance at Euryale.

"Kydoimos," Euryale said and fell into a fighting stance. "I haven't run into you in ages."

"I haven't missed you, Gorgon. Goodbye."

If Aite had a sense of elegance, Kydoimos was nothing but the embodiment of a warrior. His head and body were covered by a grey helmet and armor that was a part of him. He held sharp swords in his hands that had the air of being well-used. If Eris and Aite had stepped out of a role-playing game, Kydoimos was a raw soldier. He brandished his battered weapons. The blades gleamed in the fading sun, the edges glinting off the rays, showing that they were honed to lethal sharpness.

Then there was a noise and a buzzing sound. The figures behind the now-shadowy form of Eris. They roared something, but then there was a louder growl, and something bounded forward to halt in front of Asher.

He blinked at the sight.

His friend Lenno, also the Mishipeshu, or water-panther, now stood next to Asher, a huge dragon cat towering over the others. Then another figure coalesced next to Euryale. This one was Hebe, the juvenile goddess from Athens. Others rumbled past the crowd to stand with Euryale and Asher. He recognized Clíodhna and his mother, Roisin. His heart swelled at the sight of his kin. His mother ignored her queen who was radiating disapproval. Asher inclined his head at the banshees.

I ordered her not to come. She disobeyed me. I did not want to face the possibility of losing both of you. He stared at the goddess and then at the others.

"What are you doing here?" Asher's voice came out in a strained gasp, but he couldn't help it. A moment ago, he'd been prepared to die.

"We could not let you go into battle alone," Lenno said and the rest nodded.

The Tuatha dé Danann goddess stepped forward and faced Eris, who broke from the milling pack to face the Irish deity. Eris snarled in defiance, but a flicker of fear crossed her face.

"You do not play fair, goddess of strife. Now it is you who has a choice. Break off this insanity and end your vendetta, or this ends here."

Eris snarled. "You are outnumbered. All of my children are gods."

Clíodhna waved a dismissive hand toward the assembly of Eris's children. "They are mingin' bastards. You no longer have the element of surprise. Step away. You're a gowl, goddess or not. Leave off at once and we will call the battle a draw. Continue and we fight."

Eris raised her hands which were also now tipped with claws.

"We will never back down, Tuatha dé Danann. Now all of you will perish as well. It will be a glorious day for Eris and her multitude. Now, we attack."

* * *

Kydoimos flung himself at Euryale and she dodged to the side. He brandished his weapons and went for her again. Hebe went after Aite and the two goddesses began grappling. The other Machai joined the fray. She could not determine who went after Asher, nor who his friend Lenno was defending against. She was shocked that Lenno was participating, his dislike of her could have kept him away. She assumed they were alone in this battle, but it turned out to be the opposite.

Euryale didn't have time to wonder how their friends had gotten there or found them. That would be for later, if there was a later.

Kydoimos turned and sneered at Euryale. As the god of battlefield din and confusion, he would try to confuse her.

She waggled a finger at him. "None of your tricks, son of Eris. I am familiar with what you do."

His face was fierce with concentration, chanting something under his breath. Her mind was momentarily muddled, but Euryale shook her head and it cleared.

Then he sent a wave of confusion so powerful that she staggered back and those around her also paused. Euryale summoned her jumping power and then leaped far away from him. With another howl, Kydoimos followed her.

He may have thought he was as important, or as dominant as a Gorgon, but he was no match for her. She filled her mind with the images of her snakes, and for a moment, almost felt them on her head.

She focused on Kydoimos and opened her mouth to scream, while also penetrating him with her stare. He faltered, grey stone covering his face and then fell backward with a heavy thud.

Leaving the man behind, Euryale once again leaped into the battle scene, landing near Asher, who was battling one of the Logoi. As the children of Eris called Lies, they shifted form and were hard to get a fix on. Asher was holding his own—Asher was the son of Ares and a power in his own right.

Eris stood in the middle of the fray, watching the proceedings without engaging. It filled Euryale with rage. Euryale went to move toward the woman, and then realized she was being manipulated by yet another of her children—one of the Neikea, or Grievances. The ground was thick with bodies.

She leaped to where Asher was fighting Ponos. As she watched, he dealt the other one a fierce blow on the head and Ponos staggered back. He turned to her with a questioning air.

"It's time to use our voices, Asher. They give us the advantage."

"What advantage?" He asked the question as he dodged a dagger swipe from Ponos.

"Let's find out. We have to do it now," she said, gesturing to Hebe. The other gave her a grimace, her breathing labored as she fended off another of Eris's children, but her arm was slow to raise up. "We have to strike before anyone else gets hurt. There are still far more of them than there are of us."

Asher was panting, but he nodded. "Okay. How do you want to play this?"

She ducked away from Lethe who tried to wrench her off her feet. For a moment, she wavered, feeling Lethe's aura but then she shoved away from the other, rolling to escape Lethe's effects.

"We join forces. Fighting separately isn't working. Let's do this together. We've got nothing to lose. Right now, they are winning."

He studied the battlefield where Eris and her cohorts were decimating their party. "I'd say we've got everything to lose if this doesn't work."

She cut off his words before he could say anything further. "Then let's do this now before we lose anything—or anyone else."

"Okay."

She pointed to the battleground. "Assemble your friends."

"Will do." He raised his voice. "Bring it on, bitch! Hey, guys, a hand here?"

She reached out to Clíodhna. *Can you gather your party? We want to try something.*

Aye. I can and I will.

Then she sought Hebe. All the while, they continued to fight, battling the hordes of Eris's children. Hebe was fighting Horkos, and even though he was larger, she was holding her own. They always underestimated the teenage-looking goddess.

Asher, to me.

He came over to her, dodging the fray as he did so. She stepped away from the battle. Asher followed her, tilting his head to show his puzzlement. Then she held out her hand.

Trust me, Asher. I have a plan.

I do trust you. Let's do it.

Euryale and Asher joined hands, and she shot him a quick mental, *Are you ready?*

He nodded and they faced the others.

She leaped toward the monastery, but not even her powers were sufficient to leap all the way there, and with Asher next to her, she leaped again. Eris watched with cool detachment as they bounded away. No doubt she assumed they were abandoning the fight.

"Ready?"

"Euryale, what are we doing?"

She nodded at the battle in the distance. "I'm going to leap twice more and then we are going to come back into the mêlée. Be prepared to use your banshee voice when we arrive. You need to give every ounce of your vocal power to this. But not before I say so." She said to herself, *this had better work.* If it didn't, they were going to have far fewer friends, and the gods would mete out harsh punishment for their failure. She wasn't sure Asher would want to live if he had sent his friends and family to their deaths. She was sure he would not be given a choice.

"Gaining strength. I am not famous for my leaping abilities for nothing. Ready?"

"I supposed you might try to persuade me to leave, so I wouldn't get hurt anymore."

She took in the cut on his cheek that bled and might scar, and the wounds on his legs. "Would you?"

"No. Of course not."

"Neither would I. Come on. Let's end this."

He took up a fighting stance and gave her a thumbs up. He was a banshee and a halfling, and he was magnificent. She didn't think she could ever love anyone the way she loved him.

"Stay with me," she said and then leaped from their vantage point to another spot further away and then again, until she was hundreds of yards from the battle site.

"On my count," she said, gathering every ounce of strength in her body and in her voice. She remembered when she had learned Medusa had been slain and the numbers of times she howled at her fate. She recalled all those events and stored them in her vocal cords as memory. Asher's mind touched hers and he drew from that energy, using it to bolster his control. She fed him what she could and, together, they faced the goddess and her children.

With one ferocious leap, she plunged herself and Asher back onto the battlefield. Then they began to howl. The other banshees joined in, and even the gods who did not have sonic power contributed their voices to the din. Clíodhna stood to one side and then she, too, wailed, a pure clean sound that was an octave above the howls of the other banshees. It sent a shudder down Euryale's spine. It harmonized with Euryale's wail, giving it more potency and strength. Apart they were powerful, together they were tenfold as strong as they were separately. She shot the goddess a nod of thanks and then turned her attention to Eris.

The sounds grew. Now Lenno, Roisin, and Clíodhna added their voices to the wails of Asher and Euryale. The noise was a howl that rose and pierced the air around them. For a moment, Euryale could see Olympus and the hovering gods. Her keening filled her, continuing the wail until it was magnificent and terrible. Asher and the others keened with her, making a living wall of sound.

Lethe screamed and collapsed to her knees and stopped moving. A trickle of blood emerged from her ears. They continued wailing and then Proxis fell. Eris's face twisted and she whirled in confusion. Aite surged forward and then staggered back from the power of their blast. She, too, collapsed. Euryale didn't dare breathe or do anything other than scream. Lenno's growl was a primal thing and acted as a bass undercurrent, making their sonic blast resonate in an undercurrent that sent chills up her spine. Clíodhna's soprano gave them a four-part harmony of wailing. Euryale would have smiled if her mouth wasn't stretched in a terrible howl.

Horkos tried to charge but the sonic clout held him back.

Euryale focused on Eris, using all the remembered power of her stare to add to the cacophony around her. Eris flinched, and the woman attempted to glance away, but she could not. She did not break eye contact, as though unable to lift her gaze from Euryale's. Unfortunately, she did not turn to stone. It would have made this that much simpler. Eris vibrated, her body shaking, and those of her children who hadn't fallen, crowded around her. She turned around and around, each rotation a little quicker, a little more frantic. But she could not move; like the others, she was trapped in the aural power. Her children strained to get to her, but Lenno lunged at any who drew near. They opened their mouths, perhaps to begin their own assault, but then stared at their mother. Eris shrieked, clawing at her face. She made a terrible wail, a shrill, piercing sound that blended with their noise until it was all one thing, a wall of resonance that was fierce and unescapable. Eris rent her clothing, starting to sob as blood and ichor trickled from her ears.

Then she burst into pieces.

The shards flew out in an arc, spattering her children who came to an abrupt halt, their efforts to protect her ceasing. Lenno stopped snarling, his whiskers twitching as bits of Eris landed on him. He rumbled and shook his body, and the remnants of the goddess dropped off.

Euryale remained where she was, staring in disbelief at the scene. Where Eris had stood, there was a bit of brown that might have been her feet, followed by an arc of matter that was the remains of her.

Aite wailed and Horkos bellowed but none of her children moved. They stared at where their mother had been, unable to assimilate that she was gone.

Asher stepped forward, shielding Euryale from the carnage, but she pushed past him to go to the scene. She needed to determine for herself that the woman was gone.

"We did it," he breathed.

"We did," she agreed and regarded the assembled gods and supernatural beings. Her attention went to Eris's minions. If they were going to strike, now would be the time. Two or three of them still clustered together as though trying to assemble a counterattack, but without their leader, they were rootless.

Clíodhna faced Eris's children. "Lay off, children of the goddess, no more ructions. Do not attempt to slay any more gods and you will be safe. But mark my words. When your mother returns from this death, if you should try again, you bring death on you all. Let go this vendetta and we will not interfere with your lives. Resume, and you will be eliminated like your mother. I wager not all of you will come back from that. If you understand, leave at once. No slinjing, go right now!"

Aite hesitated, but the rest of Eris's children filed out, back toward the mainland of Crete, some glancing back to confirm that Eris was gone. Soon she, too, followed.

"Why did you let them go?" Hebe demanded, turning Clíodhna around to face her. Clíodhna shook her head and nodded at the retreating children.

"They made a hames out of the job, but we cannot slay them all. If we give them the ability to save face, then they may not be a problem again."

Hebe snorted. "They will reassemble as soon as Eris returns to the living. By not going after them, all you did was delay them. They will be back when she reappears. They have learned how to kill gods."

Euryale passed a weary hand over her eyes. "Did you have the stomach for more fighting, Hebe? They left. We won. Those are the important things."

"She's dead…" Asher said in awe. "How can we kill a goddess?"

Lenno joined them, back in his human form. He wore a pair of shorts that he must have kept on his animal self somewhere. He considered the spot where Eris's remains smoked.

"Same way they did. But ultimately, we can't," he replied. "Not for good. Just as Eris's victims will come back into being, so will she. But we dismantled her, and it will take years for her to reassemble. We will be safe, for a while."

"But not forever."

Clíodhna let out a weary sigh. "No. Not forever. It's jam on your egg to think it's over. Eris will be watched when she returns, and will not be allowed to behave the way she has. She will not have freedom for a long time, if ever. Perhaps she will be banished to an island, ala Circe. That is up to the Greeks. She is their goddess."

"We won," Asher said, his gaze going to Euryale. "We did it."

Before she could say anything, there was a fanfare and a stream of bright light hitting the beach, bathing it in a fierce glow.

Euryale gritted her teeth, the words she'd been about to say dying in her throat. As she watched, Athena, Apollo, and more of the Greek gods emerged from that shining place that she recognized as the gods' home. Mount Olympus. In the distance were columns and couches, all the accoutrements of their sanctuary that she remembered from ancient visits.

The cavalry had arrived, now that the fight was won.

Chapter Nineteen

"We have succeeded," Euryale said. Her voice didn't sound like her own, not even the recent sonic screams could account for the tremor. He tried to prod her mind, but she'd shut him out. She turned and faced the gods. Athena's face was haughty and unreadable. She was in full battle armor, which was strange considering the deed was done.

"*Skeela*. You slew the perpetrator but left her children," she said and sniffed. "I am not sure that constitutes a success."

Clíodhna stepped forward, joining Euryale, who Asher could tell was fighting not to react at being called a bitch in Greek. "They have fled. Their leader is gone. Don't slag the Gorgon. We are victorious."

"You have struck one blow. There were more to be fought, yet you did not. I do not think your Tuatha dé Danann counterparts would say you won. Unless that pantheon is less than I remember them." She paused for a moment and shook her head. "Probably the latter. So few things are what they used to be these days."

The other goddess studied the Irish one, and then dismissed her by turning her head away. Asher's blood heated. He waited for Clíodhna to do something, but all she did was incline her head, ceding the floor. She joined the others. Lenno and Hebe remained forward, glancing at each other and then at the assembled gods. But they, too, did not intervene.

He faced the major Greek goddess while sliding his hand into Euryale's. To his surprise she broke away, shaking her head. Euryale had reasons for doing everything she did. When this was over, he would tell her how he felt, but they had to get through the next few minutes.

"You used our promises to send us on this mission to kill the threat to the gods. We killed Eris and removed the threat. There is no world in which we have not fulfilled our promise. We honored our vows."

Her voice was thin with tension, its pitch a half octave higher than normal. There was a slight tremor to it, although Euryale was doing her best to hide it. Could his fierce warrior be...scared? There were many things about the former Gorgon that he had yet to understand.

Then again, she was not a former Gorgon. She was still a Gorgon. She had been one before they were turned to monsters, and even though Gorgon became synonymous with monster, it once just meant what they were. Now Euryale was still a Gorgon, and also a woman.

Athena pursed her lips and studied Asher. "You are not a part of this, son of Ares." The war god stood to the side, but he said nothing. He didn't appear happy, but he didn't challenge Athena, either. Asher's view of his absent father dipped further.

"I'm part of anything Euryale is," he returned, hoping Euryale would appreciate what he was saying.

"I do not believe you wish to share her fate."

Euryale gasped and then her body went tense. She stared at the other goddess, and then his Gorgon trembled. That Athena could affect his woman so, made Asher want to yell at the goddess and fill her with the power of his sound. He didn't think that what they had done would work on Athena, but it might wound her enough to get Euryale clear of this. This wouldn't be running away. They had done what was agreed to and their contract was complete. He and his mother should be safe. Ares was a god good to his word. Athena, though...

"Hell, I don't," he said. "Her fate is my fate."

Athena shook her head. Ares beheld his son with a faint aura of respect.

"You do not share this one. The bargain is not fulfilled. Any pact between us is null and void. I have no reason to allow Euryale to stay in human form. My wrath is not yet at an end."

"Athena, no!" Asher said, horrified at the implication of her words. He started toward the dais where the gods stood, but an invisible force field held him back. He struggled against it, but couldn't take one more step closer. It was like he had immense gravity under his feet, making it impossible to move.

"I knew you would renege," Euryale said, tossing her hair and standing in the sand, her back straight and her chin lifted. She raised to her full height and folded her arms. "It is no surprise that you played me false. You have never been an honorable goddess."

"You dare!" Athena spat out the words. Her hands filled with a bright light and she flung it at Euryale. His woman didn't try to shift, she didn't try to evade, all she did was stand there and accept the strike. Even as Asher stumbled backward, released from the power keeping him frozen, she stood there.

Then Euryale cried out the most horrible sound, the sonic boom piercing the sky. It was as powerful as the blast from before, but this was a howl of rage and despair. She covered her face with her hands and fell to the sand.

As he watched, she changed, her skin thickening and turning a dull green, her hair becoming snakes that were reddish-brown in color, all of them hissing as they appeared. Talons sprouted from her nails and her face distorted, her nose and teeth growing, fangs sprouting in her mouth. Her legs lost their shape and merged into a snake form, growing behind her until she was seven feet long.

Euryale let out an earsplitting shriek that went on and on. She stretched to her full length on her tail, towering over the assembled people and continuing to screech. She howled and then began moving toward them, the snakes that were now her hair a collective mass that pointed straight toward the gathered people.

It's not fair. I did everything she asked. It's not fair.

Asher moved in front of her and reached out his arm. She got closer and it took everything he had not to jump back out of her path. This was the Gorgon in full regalia, as terrifying as any legend. Now he understood why she had been so feared all these years. As a goddess in human form, she was powerful and frightening in her own right, but as a monster, she was fearsome beyond measure. If he hadn't been familiar with the essence of her, he would have run and prayed he could get somewhere safe before she found him. But there was no running from this one. If she hunted you, it would only be a matter of time before she found you and ended you.

Asher accepted the fact that he might be about to die.

"Euryale, no," he said and waited. She drew all the way up to him, her snakes within a hair's breadth of his face…and stopped.

He wasn't sure if she understood who he was for long moments. She studied him in puzzlement and then slid back a foot and murmured something to the snakes. To his relief they calmed, although a few of them still hissed. She could turn men to stone in this form if she wished, and yet he peered at her. Then he held out his hand to her, ignoring the sharp claws.

It's not fair it's not fair it's not fair.

I will make it right.

Euryale took his hand. Hers was scaly and rough, and it didn't matter. This was his woman, in any form she was in. He turned to face Ares and Athena.

"Change her back." He addressed Athena but also turned his attention to his father.

"I will not," Athena said, holding her shield and one of Zeus's thunderbolts.

"Athena, you are not being fair," Ares said, but his voice trailed off. For a god of war, he was meek next to the angry woman by his side. In ancient tales, Athena was supposed to be the cool-headed one, while Ares was spoiling for a fight, but from all appearances, the opposite was true.

"It was not right that their sister soiled herself in my temple, and with Poseidon, no less," Athena retorted.

"Jesus, Mary and Joseph," Clíodhna said, stepping up next to him but giving Euryale a wide berth. "You are a melter. That was thousands of years ago. You must have something better to do with your time than nurse this old grudge."

"You know what they say about the *old* gods," Hebe said, flanking them on Euryale's side, showing no fear of the hissing snakes. He supposed that was how it must have been in the days after they were transformed. "Those *old timers* can't let things go. It's bad for your blood pressure, goddess. Just drop it, give E here back her face and let's be done with this. You're being vindictive and stupid. Sure, that's your gig, but it's not a good look on you. It makes you appear ancient. Maybe your time is up, old hag."

Athena hefted the thunderbolt, aiming it at Hebe before lowering it again.

"She will not relent, son," Ares said. "Step away from the Gorgon and let her go. Her fate is no longer entwined with yours."

He had only moments before she reacted. Grabbing Euryale's hands and ignoring the bite of her talons in his skin, Asher kissed each claw-tipped finger and gazed into her eyes. He waited for the moment when he would turn to stone, but it didn't come.

"Her fate is linked to mine," Asher replied and turned to face his father. "It doesn't matter what form she's in. Euryale is the woman I love, and whether she's woman or monster, I will stay with her."

"You would stay with her even if she is a fiend?" Ares spat the words, and rubbed his beard with rapid strokes in a gesture that suggested it was something he did when he was agitated.

Athena let out a disgusted noise. "She's a beast, son of Ares. She's been a brute for longer than she was a goddess."

Asher shook his head. "So what? You're gods. You are eternal. You condemned her and her sisters to this life because you were insulted. Well, no more. She did as you asked. She solved your mystery and Eris has been neutralized. Now fulfill your promise. Change her back!"

Athena turned her back on Asher. Euryale growled, a low, menacing sound. Her snakes hissed at the same time, and for a moment, fear surged through Asher. This wasn't his Euryale. This other side of her was as much a part of her as his having two parents from different pantheons. She was his goddess, his Euryale, and she was also this thing.

Athena and Ares huddled together for several moments and then the goddess turned back to him. She grew and flooded with light. Euryale hissed at her and tried to lunge forward, but Asher held onto her hand. If she strained to free herself, he couldn't stop her. Euryale was stronger than him. But she didn't. His heart soared at that realization. She was her monster self, but there was something inside her that was still Euryale.

"I will not return her to her goddess state. Your puny concerns are of no importance to me. You cannot harm me, you simple-minded banshee, even if you are the son of Ares. Your wishes are of little concern."

"But I can. And I will. I will challenge all who do not honor their vows."

Clíodhna stood there, now dressed in a green floor-length gown. Her hair which had been tied into plaits, was unbound and tumbled down her back. Her gown was gathered at the shoulders and waist, and for a moment, Asher had the impression of birds around her, but he blinked, and that notion was gone. The Queen of the Banshees was as regal and as otherworldly as Athena. As he watched, Clíodhna expanded to a greater height, matching Athena's.

"You?" Athena asked in disbelief. "You dare threaten me, Queen of the Banshees, member of the Tuatha dé Danann? Your pantheon is nothing to me. You are minor gods, and I am Athena. You are of no concern to one such as me."

Clíodhna beckoned to Asher and Euryale. She appeared confused but went with him when Asher tugged on her hand. Her snakes, however, turned to face Athena and hissed at her. Euryale's body was stiff. He had mere moments before her bestial side broke free. He suspected it was the goddess who still lived in her memory that was the reason she hadn't acted. Soon she would plunge at the woman who was her tormentor…and Asher would join her. Loathing for Athena swelled in him, and he didn't care about any consequences. He would get his revenge on this bitch of a goddess who dared to take his love away from him.

"I care little what a manky goddess like you thinks of me," Clíodhna said with a shrug. "False words, no matter who they are from, are still false. I have something that you don't have."

Athena raised her lips in a sneer, and for a moment, Asher thought she was going to strike at the assembled people right then and there.

"What is that?" Athena's attention turned to Asher. He crossed his arms and glared at her, uncaring if that was foolhardy. She had taken Euryale from him, and he would go down fighting if he had to in order to make it right.

"I have honor," the Queen of the Banshees responded. "I have dignity and you are nothing but an oath breaker. I believe one of the Machai has the right to call you on this. Perhaps I should summon them back?"

Athena snarled. "You are nothing but a footnote in history. I am Athena. What do you have? Nothing."

"You are without integrity. You call this one a monster, like, but you are the one who condemned her to that fate. Who is the monster, the one created, or the one who created her? Your grievances have no place in today. You ask what is on my side, and I will show you."

The ground behind her shimmered as Clíodhna released what Asher understood had been a glamour. Those who fought with them remained, but there were more people in the field. There were dozens of minor Greek gods and members of the Tuatha dé Danann. A man he felt was named Neit was in that mix, as well as Badb, one of his wives. Prende and Enji were there. All in all, there were over a hundred beings, gods, and supernaturals alike who now stood there facing Athena and Ares. It had to be an illusion, but nonetheless tears pricked his sight at the crowd.

Clíodhna gestured to the assemblage. "These are the ones who would speak for Euryale and Asher. There is no tripe here, no, as you say, bullshit. Asher and Euryale removed the threat of Eris and her children, at your bidding. Whether those children are dangers in the future is irrelevant. You are thick if you think to play them false. They did your bidding and you repay them with treachery. That is not worthy of a goddess, Athena. I should not need to tell you that."

Euryale hissed, followed by her snakes. Asher had mere moments before she struck. With two major members of the pantheon here, that had one ending—disaster. Yet, it would be fitting to let go of her hand and allow her to take her vengeance on the goddess who had wronged her twice.

Do not let her go, son. Control her for a little while longer. We will deal with this.

Clíodhna met his gaze. He glanced at Euryale, whose snakes were moving back and forth on her head. Her talons dug into his skin, but he didn't let go. Not yet.

I will try.

"These are but mere illusions, projections of others. They can do nothing. I do not care what the goddess of a minor pantheon thinks of me," Athena said and gave Asher and Euryale a cold stare. "You deserve to be a monster for what your sister did."

Prende rolled her eyes. The resemblance between her and the Irish goddess was apparent in their beauty. She gave Athena a cool stare.

"You are still yammering about that after how many millennia? You are supposed to be a goddess of wisdom, but you are no wiser than the lowest fool. Nasreddin Hodja often told foolish jokes and was a laughingstock to many, but he was a thousand times smarter than you."

Asher was unfamiliar with the person Prende was talking about, but the scorn in her voice made him wince. Euryale coiled beside him.

"You dare compare me to your story-telling fool in folklore?" Athena appeared ready to lunge at Prende.

All this time, Ares remained on the dais, his appearance a study in misery. Still he did nothing. Asher's respect for his father continued to plummet. He could stop this but chose not to.

"I do," Prende said. "I point out that there is no greater fool than the one who refuses to see reason. Nasreddin is a charming man and his stories bring joy to all who hear them. What is your reasoning for behaving in such an unkind and capricious manner? You are a goddess and you have a responsibility, yet you let old grudges rule you. This is not worthy of you. Perhaps you are what you appear to be. Petty and irrational."

Euryale broke free of him and he let her go. She pivoted, hissing, her snakes following, and flexed her talons. She opened her mouth and emitted a bloodcurdling scream, the sonic pitch so high, that it was at the upper register of his hearing.

Athena grinned as though she'd hoped for this moment to happen. Asher understood in a flash. If Euryale attacked, then Athena would have an excuse to kill her. He turned to his father, prepared to defend the woman he loved against these gods. It would fail, of course, but that wasn't important. He was about to die—that also didn't matter. Trying to protect Euryale against the injustice done to her was the only thing that was important.

"Damn it, Euryale, no!"

Chapter Twenty

She hissed as the beast settled deep inside her. Euryale had been in the form for a few minutes, but it was as familiar as an old coat. Her snakes hissed on her head, and she welcomed their writhing. She listened to all the petty ramblings of the people around her, but there was one thing on her mind: Kill Athena. Strike her down and take her head as Perseus had once taken Medusa's. She had just dispatched Eris and her children, she could do this.

"Euryale, no!"

She knew that voice. She liked that voice, loved the person using it. None of that mattered at the moment. The thing that was important was getting revenge on this cold bitch of a goddess who played with her life. She was as big a monster as she had turned Euryale into, for she acted without honor.

"Asher, stay out of this," she said with the part of her that was still thinking like the goddess she had been moments before. "This is between me and Athena."

Her voice held a sibilant quality. It wouldn't be long before speech was difficult. She was in an in-between place where she was once again a monster but still remembered a bit of the other. It wouldn't last long.

"The hell it is," Asher said.

She had been about to run toward Athena, but she paused. She turned to study the assembled people. There were at least a dozen gods and more banshees and shifters. A Vila hovered above the fray, green grass growing under her feet. Were they all here for her? For Asher? She cocked her head and met Clíodhna's gaze.

"I will handle this, Gorgon," Clíodhna said and raised her hands. "Gods and goddesses, to me."

To her surprise, Ares stepped down from the dais and joined the others. Within moments, the gods were at the front next to the Queen of the Banshees, and the rest behind.

"Ares, you dare?" Athena asked, her face a mask of fury.

"I do." When his gaze went to Euryale, there was compassion in it. She didn't want to credit it, but even as her humanity slipped away, she detected what she would have called regret if she were still in her other form.

The relationship with Asher was over, of course. There was no way a half god and a monster could sustain a liaison. She hoped she remembered the way she loved him when she reverted. It would be so nice to recollect what it was like to love and be loved by someone other than her sisters. But there was no future for them. They would part here. For that, as well as the rest, Athena would pay.

Even as her humanity faded, Euryale marched toward Athena, and opened her mouth. She would kill this bitch, or die trying. She had nothing left to lose.

* * *

Euryale started to move. It was too late. She wasn't powerful enough to defeat Athena. He looked at Lenno, and his father, and the gods and banshees who had joined them at the end. He would miss all of them.

"Euryale, wait," he said. "I will help."

Her snakes hissed but her face cleared. His Euryale was still in there, his beautiful Gorgon. Even under the green skin and talons, the woman he loved was visible.

"Asher," she said, her fangs making the 's' hiss out like her snakes. "I have no future. You do. This bitch will pay."

"I will kill you where you stand, Gorgon," Athena said, grasping her spear in her right hand. With her left, she raised the shield with her face etched into it and covered her own visage. "You and your sisters do not deserve to live."

With a hiss, Euryale charged toward Athena. Athena elevated her weapon and aimed it at Euryale.

From behind him, hundreds of wails exploded, the fierce keening of the banshees. At the same time, Lenno snarled, shifted into his water-panther, and began charging toward Athena. Enji's hands erupted into flames, and he flung fire bolts at her shield. A feeling of wellness flowed over Asher—perhaps that was Prende's influence. Clíodhna continued to stir the banshees, and their cries reached screeching proportions until his eardrums might burst.

Both Euryale and Asher stopped and watched in amazement as Athena's spear shattered in mid-flight. Ares threw his spear at Athena. It struck her in the helmet, sending her staggering back. She picked up the fallen thunderbolt and hurled it toward Euryale and Asher.

It left her hand and hung in midair, crackling at the ends. Athena gaped, and the banshees fell silent on a signal from Clíodhna. All activity ceased. Asher went next to Euryale and stood facing Athena and the motionless thunderbolt.

"It may be that Eris's lesson is not enough to strike down a major god," Clíodhna said with the manner of someone discussing the weather. "But are you willing to take that chance? Many of us have learned today what it takes to kill a god. Are you so eager to have the theory tested?"

Everything went still for long moments. The thunderbolt quivered where it hovered in the air, mere inches away from Euryale.

"You dare?"

"I am not slagging you," the Tuatha dé Danann goddess said. "It is you who is forcing my hand. We should be collaborating, not tearing each other apart. Restore Euryale to her promised form and we can parlay. This threat involves all of us."

Nothing moved except for the wind high up in the trees. Everyone had the air of being frozen like the thunderbolt, but it was nothing more than the assembly holding their breath. Whether real or illusion, the others behind the goddess had power and weight to their stance.

Then there was another bright light. Asher threw up his hand to shield his face, and for a moment, nothing but brilliance surrounded him.

Euryale let out a wail and Asher turned to her in alarm. Her snakes were melting away and her skin was returning to normal. Her talons and fangs receded. Within moments, she was in her human body again. She cried out at the sight of her goddess form and her gaze went to Asher. That he was the first person she thought to take into consideration filled him with unspeakable happiness.

Athena pushed at the thunderbolt, but it continued to hang in the air. Ares chuckled. Then Clíodhna joined in. So did the others, until the entire assembly was laughing.

"You *dare?*" she asked again, and another spear materialized in her hand. Before she could throw it, it crumbled.

A voice boomed out of the sky.

"You go too far, daughter," the voice said, and a man appeared by the thunderbolt. "You have been blinded by your hatred. You dare use my weapons for your own selfish ends, Athena? I will not allow it."

If Asher had any preconceived notions of what Zeus's appearance would be, they were dispelled in that moment. The god who gripped the thunderbolt—his weapon—was tall, taller even than Asher, with the sort of face that sent hearts fluttering around the world. He was so striking that the gathering gasped.

Zeus breathed on the thunderbolt and it vanished, to appear as a bit of itself in a belt on his tight-fitting jeans. Athena stood motionless, staring at her father and then at Euryale.

"You have let your petty jealousy rule you for far too long. This Gorgon has served us well. You do her a disservice by transforming her back into beast. I have restored her." He glared at Athena and his gaze was fierce. "I should punish you. I should send you down to Tartarus for a millennium in punishment for your arrogance."

Athena blanched, an expression he had never expected he would witness on the goddess. "Father, I…"

He sighed. "I should punish you, but you are still my daughter. Get out of my sight."

Athena vanished, taking her shield but leaving the shattered remains of her spear.

Asher pulled Euryale to him and held her close, reveling in her warm body. Her hair still felt serpentine and there was a faint hiss when he drew her to him. Perhaps the snakes weren't quite absorbed into her. Perhaps they never would be.

A short moment later, Euryale was hugging him back, her arms tight around him, her head buried against his shoulder. Her body shook as slow tears rolled down her cheeks. That his strong, capable woman could be driven to tears, made Asher want to follow Athena to Mount Olympus and hurt her…kill her.

"Euryale," Zeus said, and pushed his palm toward them. Asher's body surged forward, and they began sliding toward the leader of the Greek pantheon, despite the fact that their feet weren't moving. Euryale continued to cling to him, wiping her face on his shirt as they slid across the ground.

When they reached the other god, they stopped, and Euryale stepped out of Asher's embrace to face Zeus. Asher released her, even though every instinct was telling him to step in front of her and shield her. It was conceivable that Zeus had sent Athena away to slaughter Euryale himself. Anything was possible with the Greeks.

"You will leave off this one," the Queen of the Banshees said, her attention on Zeus.

To Asher's surprise, the other god nodded. "It is as you say, Clíodhna. We need to work toward a common goal. This threat now involves all of us. I cannot say what would have happened if you had continued. It is something we all must focus on." He grinned and his radiance shone around them. "May I say, you are fetching tonight. As are you, Prende," he hastened to add. The Albanian goddess said nothing, but a faint smile played on her face. She glanced at Euryale and Asher, and then she and Enji turned and vanished as Athena had moments before.

Euryale knelt, bowing her head before Zeus. Asher's mouth fell open when she bent her knee to the man. Sure, he was the Greek god leader but still…she was Euryale.

"Rise, Gorgon," Zeus said with a magnanimous air.

"Thank you, oh, great Zeus," she said.

Euryale?

I'm learning. I need allies.

"You may think sweet words will sway us, but they will not," Clíodhna said with a stern voice. She moved closer. "A terrible thing was done to this woman. It is only right that you fixed that, but there is no guarantee it will not happen again. It is, how do the Americans say it, that Athena has had a bug up her ass this entire time. If you are fannying about with the next mortal who takes your fancy, who will stop her from playing Euryale false again?"

Zeus clutched a hand to his heart, his muscles rippling with the movement. Everything he did was designed to draw the eye to the perfection of his form. Even Asher couldn't help but notice how handsome of a man he was. He was more than movie-star perfect; he was ethereal.

"You wound me, Clíodhna," he said with the continued amused air. "You also underestimate me. You spoke true when you said this threat involves us all. For that reason, I have made things right. Now I charge you with discovering how to combat it. I will make you a bargain, Queen of the Banshees. Come visit me in Mount Olympus, and I will ensure that Athena is never again permitted to transform this one into a monster."

"My sisters, too," Euryale insisted.

"Ah, your sisters," Zeus said with a distracted tone. "Stheno, yes, I will also do this for her. But not for Medusa. She has her own destiny. The two of you were pawns in this battle, but she was the instigator. She is not part of this."

"No way," Euryale said and Clíodhna emitted a sigh.

"You may be a goddess, Gorgon, but I am Queen of the Banshees and I make my own bargains. I accept your proposal, Zeus. I've long fancied seeing Mount Olympus for myself. I wish to taste your ambrosia. We don't have such things among the Tuatha dé Danann."

"Zeus, Medusa too," Euryale said, as though forgetting that she had moments ago said she needed allies.

"No," he replied. "Stheno was as innocent as you and did not deserve her fate. I have long regretted what happened with the two of you. You are immortals like us, but your sister is different. Have you not wondered why Athena was so angry? Perhaps there is more to Medusa's story than she told you. She must come to terms with her choices. You and your sister, however, are free."

Asher pushed on Euryale with his mind when it appeared she was going to argue further. She gave him a strained glance but shut her mouth. He breathed out a sigh of relief. He had gotten his Gorgon back.

Clíodhna blushed when Zeus held out a hand to her.

"I will be with you in a tetch," she said and turned back to address her people.

"Euryale," Asher said and embraced her again. She was restored to him. He felt the warmth of her body and reveled in her touch.

Clíodhna joined Zeus after raising a hand in final farewell to her people. The banshees were already dispersing, vanishing as the Vila and the others did. In the end, they were an illusion but a good one. Ares, Lenno, and Hebe stayed behind. Without these people, his precious Gorgon would still be a monster, but he couldn't wait to be alone with her. There was much he needed to say.

* * *

"I shall take my leave," Ares said, clapping Asher on the back and then paused. "But first, you should know something of your heritage." As he said the words, Asher's face paled. "I am sure you have often wondered of the mysteriousness surrounding your birth. It is true that I struck a bargain with your mother, but you are more god than banshee. A quarter banshee to be exact. It was the only way to produce a male." Ares met Asher's gaze and clutched his shoulders. "I am proud of you, son." Asher did not say a word, only stared after his father in what appeared to be disbelief.

Ares rose and Euryale breathed out a covert sigh of relief.

Asher gave his father a hug. The god clasped his son to him and then glanced over at Euryale. She stood still for a moment, her face blank, turning her head to meet his eyes. Then he beckoned her over and Euryale joined them, touching the Greek god of war while she pressed her chest against the man she loved.

Then Ares raised a hand. There was a tragic sort of grin on his face. He seemed to have many things that he was keeping to himself, but Euryale was just as shocked as Asher appeared by this new revelation. The talk of parentage could wait for another time. It had never seemed to be an issue with him before. All she craved was for Ares to be gone so she could be alone with Asher. She was restored to her old self, her goddess status no longer in question.

The lights of Heraklion gleamed over the island. In the distance, the Aegean Sea glimmered in the moonlight, the waves dancing over the shore. She wondered if Poseidon was out there. He had not put in an appearance today, even though it was his mischief that had started this in the first place.

It took hours after Zeus restored her and the gods faced off to settle all other matters so she and Asher could be alone. Hours of visiting with his goddess and their friends and catching up on all things Eris and the crazy events of the last week. His mother hugged them both, and if her embrace of Euryale was a little cool, the Gorgon understood. Things were different now and would never go back to the way they were.

Hebe spent some time with them, along with Lenno. Euryale detected a spark between the goddess and Asher's dour water-panther friend. Hebe was welcome to the guy as long as he left her alone. She doubted she and Lenno would ever be friends. Then again, there was no telling what the future held. She did miss her snakes, though, they had been her companions for centuries. Even understanding they were still a part of her did not mean she couldn't mourn them a little.

After the last of them left, she led Asher back to the sofa. The waves lapped against the shore outside their window in low rhythmic sounds, their tides a sort of melody.

"Athena won't forget this insult," Euryale warned, and Asher groaned.

"You heard Zeus. She can't harm you again. He forbade it."

"She could very well try something else. Medusa is still vulnerable."

"You love your sisters very much, don't you?"

She nodded. "They love me back. It distressed Stheno not to be here but she is a warrior. She understands the power of oaths. If I had recognized what Clíodhna was going to do, though…" She let her voice trail off. "If Athena had killed me, though, she would have had Stheno to answer to."

"I like her already. I have nothing but sisters, if you count all the banshees who are related to me. Still, there's nothing like relatives. I want to meet your sisters. I want to learn everything there is about you and them."

"I do love them," she said and laced her fingers together. Now that the moment was here, the words twisted inside her like a pretzel, rendering her inarticulate.

"Damn it, Euryale…" he began and then he, too, fell silent. They stared at each other for a moment, and then she cleared her throat.

"I love them," she said. They had been through so much, and now that it was over, she had to act.

"I love them," she said again. "But I love you more."

He blinked. "You…do?"

She had envisioned him throwing his arms up and declaring his love again, but all he did was remain still. He must have said what he said in the courtyard to get the Greek gods off his back. It was not the reaction she had hoped for, but it was too late to turn back now. "I do. I have loved you for a while, since Ireland, but I didn't dare speak it in case Athena turned me back into a monster. I couldn't burden you with that. Now I am free to say it. I love you, Asher. I love the god part of you and the banshee part of you and everything in between. When I was a goddess, I was as proud as the Olympians, but millennia of being a monster taught me humility. I love you, and even if you don't love me back, I had to say it."

She almost backed away from his lack of motion and then did push away. His mind was closed to her. She had miscalculated. Asher might like her, desire her, but he didn't love her. His words to Ares and Athena had been a lie. Her heart fell, and she swallowed against a mouth gone dry with the crushing blow. She would survive it. She had survived worse.

"You can't love me," he said, astonishment written on his face. "It's not possible."

She may be in female form again, a goddess restored, but the beast flared at that. She could feel the snakes pulse inside her. They would always be there for her. Her snakes and her sisters were, in the end, the only things she could count on.

"Oh, I am sorry, Asher. I didn't realize you were too good for a former monster to love."

He opened his mouth, but no sound came out. Her emotions, flying so high a moment before, continued to plummet by his unexpected reaction. The least he could have done was let her down easy, instead of sitting there like someone had crawled into his house and died.

She would find her way home. Screw the stuff in Los Angeles, she would not go back to the United States. Perhaps she would spend some time with Stheno or go to some other country. The one thing she didn't want to do was stay where a banshee couldn't discern what to say to her.

She turned to leave. As she rushed for the door, he bounded after her. He placed a hand on the doorknob and faced her.

"Euryale, stop. You surprised me, that's all."

She was a goddess. She was a monster. She was powerful and strong, and she could do this. The world was tiny when you were a deity, but not so little that you couldn't avoid someone if you didn't want to be around them. There were many pantheons and supernatural beings who would welcome her. She would avoid Ireland and Greece and go somewhere where she could forget all about that wretched pantheon and banshee who made her heart and mind sing.

"Euryale, stop. Give me a moment to take it in."

She didn't want to give him an instant. Hurt and fury blazed in her body and on her reddened face. She hadn't told anyone but her sisters she loved them for centuries, and the humiliation would be burned in her mind for a long time.

"What is there to take in? I told you how I felt. You didn't reply. Fine. I'm used to people not wanting to be around me. But if you'll let go of the door, I'll get out of your life and we can pretend this moment never happened."

"I never said I didn't want to be with you," he said and released the door. But before she could bolt through it, he grabbed her and enclosed her in a hug, enveloping her with his body.

"You didn't say you did, either," she said, ashamed that her voice shook. This wasn't like her. She should be in better control of herself than this.

"You sprang it on me. I didn't expect it."

She remained stiff in his arms and then began to relax. Euryale closed her arms around his back and leaned against him, emotions close to the surface. She hadn't cried in centuries. Yet she could feel moisture gathering on her lashes that was threatening to spill down.

They stood together for several minutes, not saying anything, before Asher drew back and tilted her face to meet his with one gentle press of his finger. She should have resisted, but instead she let him turn her face up to his.

Her breath caught. All the emotions she had been hoping for were shining in his countenance. Her ruined heart began beating with hope.

"Asher?" she asked, and her voice trembled. Later she would be strong, but she wasn't feeling it right now. She was needy, emotional, wretched, and glorious all at the same time.

"Ah, hell, Euryale, I always imagined when I told a woman I loved her that it would be over flowers and candlelight. Well," he said, and his voice was rueful, "I've done that in the past, but that woman was never you. I hoped for a better time, a more romantic setting, but you gods do things as you will. I love you back, Euryale, Gorgon, love of my life. There's never been anyone like you. There never *will* be anyone like you again."

Euryale trembled; she couldn't help it. So many emotions coursed through her system at once that she believed she would overflow. One thing broke through the myriad notions.

He loved her.

"Say it again," she said, unable to keep the plaintive tone from her voice. All the lonely years burst inside her. Her body was trembling so hard with the aftermath of feeling. Asher wrapped her in his arms again. She touched the strength of him, the muscles and the skin and his beating heart that was, if his words were true, hers.

"I love you," he said, his words muffled against her hair. "Euryale, are you okay? You're shaking."

She breathed out against his shirt and raised her head. "I assumed you didn't love me," she admitted. She would have to start sharing things, what she was doing and feeling, and all the ways that two people interacted. Asher was worth it.

"You're a goddess and a Gorgon and so many amazing things. There was no way someone like you could love someone like me. I was prepared for you to say goodbye and head out, not to tell me you loved me. Euryale, I love you so much. I think Ireland is where I fell in love with you, too. You're the woman I *have* to have in my life. It doesn't matter what form that takes. I love you."

She kissed him then. It was still unbelievable. She had spent centuries as an outcast and now this. She was a goddess doomed to be a monster who had saved the gods, and this was her reward. Athena had put them together with no idea what she had created. He was hers.

"My Euryale. My own," he said and touched her cheek with shaking fingers. She wasn't the only one caught in strong emotions. It warmed her heart that had been about to grow cold. The rest of the world didn't matter as long as she had Asher.

"And you're mine, Asher," she said and turned her head so he could caress her face. She sought to bathe in his touch.

"Yes. I'm yours." He brushed a kiss over her lips, holding her chin for his caress. "There's nobody else for me. Just you, my beautiful, complicated Gorgon. Euryale, will you come be with me? In Los Angeles, I mean. I've got some things in motion that I could leave, but I'd rather finish them first. If you don't want to, we can figure something else out, but if you have nowhere in particular to go, why not give L.A. a try? If you don't like it later, we can talk."

She pretended to consider, her face slanted away from Asher. Then she faced him. "Your friend doesn't like me."

He appeared to recognize the "yes" in her soul. "I have a feeling he might be preoccupied with a certain goddess of youth for a while. He'll come to like you, as he spends time with you. He's a strong power and I think he's threatened."

"Too bad."

"Yes, it is."

She brushed another kiss over his lips and sighed with pleasure. "I don't need to hide anymore. I am willing to try Los Angeles, Asher, although I am iffy about it as a permanent location."

"We can buy land. I hear there are areas near San Diego where we could find a place that has caves."

Euryale laughed, a tinkling sound. "That's not necessary. My cave days are done. But I wouldn't mind a home away from Los Angeles."

"Whatever you want, my love, just say it and I'll make it happen."

My love. The words filled her with light. A day ago, she understood the world—her world—would end, and now she had everything she desired. For a woman who had spent millennia without hope, this feeling was so new, it was gossamer-thin, like dandelion seeds bobbing in the wind. But she, like the dandelion, survived.

"Asher, can we get married?"

He blinked. "What? Marriage?"

Her fragile heart sank again but his face broke into a radiant, joyful grin.

"Is that what you want?" he continued. "But you're an ancient goddess, human needs don't apply to you."

"Marriage is an ancient custom," she said. "I want to call you husband. Will you?"

He nodded. "Of course. I want to have you as my wife for the rest of my life."

"That will be long."

"So much the better."

When he kissed her, it was a kiss of promise, and of passion, and of all the days to come. It told her without words that he loved her and would be by her side in all the adventures to come. She had a new life to live, and a man to share it. She couldn't ask for anything else.

"Come on," he said and raised his eyebrows toward the other room. "We have a lot to celebrate. I want to show you how much I love you. Will you let me?"

There was one answer, and it covered so many things.

"Yes," she said and took his hand to lead him to the bedroom. "Yes. Now and forever."

THE END

About the Author

USA Today Bestselling author Claire Davon has written on and off for most of her life, starting with fan fiction when she was very young. She writes across a wide range of genres, and does not consider any of it off limits or out of reach. If a story calls to her, she will write it. She currently lives in Los Angeles and spends her free time writing novels and short stories, as well as doing animal rescue and enjoying the sunshine. Claire's website is www.clairedavon.com.

Interested in learning more about Claire and her stories? Signing up for her newsletter is easy! Just go to: clairedavon.com/newsletter and you will have access to news, as well as giveaways and special bonus content only available to her subscribers!

Look for these titles by Claire Davon

Now Available:

Elementals' Challenge
Fire Danger
Air Attack
Water Fall

Beyond Elementals' Challenge
A Whisker of Fire

Shifter Wars
No Ordinary Fairy

Universe Chronicles
Shifting Auras
Tracking Shadows

Standalones
The Mormo's Protection